The Ancient
Vampire . . .

I am a vampire. Blood does not bother me. I like blood. Even seeing my own blood does not frighten me. But what my blood can do to others—to the whole world for that matter—terrifies me. Once God made me take a vow to create no more vampires. Once I believed in God. But my belief, like my vow, has been shattered too many times in my long life. I am Alisa Perne, the now-forgotten Sita, child of a demon. I am the oldest living creature on earth.

For orders other than by individual consumers, Pocket Books grants a discount on the purchase of 10 or more copies of single titles for special markets or premium use. For further details, please write to the Vice-President of Special Markets, Pocket Books, 1633 Broadway, New York, NY 10019-6785, 8th Floor.

For information on how individual consumers can place orders, please write to Mail Order Department, Simon & Schuster, Inc., 200 Old Tappan Road, Old Tappan, NJ 07675.

Christopher PIKE

The Last Vampire 3
RED DICE

AN ARCHWAY PAPERBACK
Published by POCKET BOOKS
New York   London   Toronto   Sydney   Tokyo   Singapore

This book is a work of fiction. Names, characters, places and incidents are products of the author's imagination or are used fictitiously. Any resemblance to actual events or locales or persons, living or dead, is entirely coincidental.

AN ARCHWAY PAPERBACK *Original*

 An Archway Paperback published by
POCKET BOOKS, a division of Simon & Schuster Inc.
1230 Avenue of the Americas, New York, NY 10020

ISBN: 0-671-87268-0

First Archway Paperback printing May 1995

10 9 8 7 6 5

AN ARCHWAY PAPERBACK and colophon are registered trademarks of Simon & Schuster Inc.

Stepback art by Danilo Ducak

Printed in the U.S.A.

IL 14+

For Rene

RED DICE

1

I am a vampire. Blood does not bother me. I like blood. Even seeing my own blood does not frighten me. But what my blood can do to others—to the whole world for that matter—terrifies me. Once God made me take a vow to create no more vampires. Once I believed in God. But my belief, like my vow, has been shattered too many times in my long life. I am Alisa Perne, the now-forgotten Sita, child of a demon. I am the oldest living creature on earth.

I awake in a living room smelling of death. I watch as my blood trickles through a thin plastic tube into the arm of Special Agent Joel Drake, FBI. He now lives as a vampire instead of the human being he was when he closed his eyes. I have broken my promise to Lord Krishna—Joel did not ask me to make him a vampire. Indeed, he told me not to, to let him die in peace. But I did not listen. Therefore, Krishna's protection, his grace, no longer applies to me. Perhaps it is good. Perhaps I will die soon. Perhaps not.

I do not die easily.

I remove the tubing from my arm and stand. At my feet lies the body of Mrs. Fender, mother of Eddie Fender, who also lies dead, in a freezer at the end of the hall. Eddie had been a vampire, a very powerful one, before I cut off his head. I step over his mother's body to search for a clock. Somehow, fighting the forces of darkness, I have misplaced my watch. A clock ticks in the kitchen above the stove. Ten minutes to twelve. It is dark outside.

I have been unconscious for almost twenty-four hours.

Joel will awaken soon, I know, and then we must go. But I do not wish to leave the evidence of my struggle with Eddie for the FBI to examine. Having seen how Eddie stole and used the blood of my creator, Yaksha, I know I must vaporize this sick house. My sense of smell is acute, as is my hearing. The pump that cools the large freezer in the back is not electric but powered by gasoline. I smell large amounts of fuel on the back porch. After I toss the gasoline all over the house, and wake Joel, I will strike a match. Fire pleases me, although it has the power to destroy me. Had I not been a vampire, I might have become a pyromaniac.

The gasoline is stored in two twenty-gallon steel tanks. Because I have the strength of many men, I have no trouble lifting them both at once. Yet even I am surprised by how light they feel. Before I passed out, I was like Joel, on the verge of death. Now I am stronger than I can ever remember being. There is a reason. Yaksha gave me what blood he had left in his veins before I buried him in the sea. He gave me his power, and I never realized how great it was until this moment. It is a wonder I was able to defeat Eddie, who also drank from Yaksha. Perhaps Krishna came to my aid, one last time.

I take the drums into the living room. From the freezer, I remove Eddie's body, severed head, and even the hard blood on the freezer floor. I pick them all up and place them on my living room barbecue. Next I begin to break up the couch and tables into easy-to-burn pieces. The noise causes Joel to stir but he does not waken. Newborn vampires sleep deep and wake up hungry. I wonder if Joel will be like my beloved Ray, reluctant to drink from the living. I hope not. I loved Ray above all things, but as a vampire, he was a pain in the ass.

I think of Ray.

He has been dead less than two days.

"My love," I whisper. "My sorrow."

There is no time for grief; there never is. There is no time for joy, I think bitterly. Only for life, pain, death. God did not plan this creation. It was a joke to him, a dream. Once, in a dream, Krishna told me many secrets. But he may have lied to me. It would have been like him.

I am almost done throwing the fuel around and

tearing up the house when I hear the sound of approaching cars. There are no sirens but I know these are police cruisers. Police drive differently from normal people, worse actually. They drive faster and the officers in these squad cars are anxious to get here. I have incredibly sensitive hearing—I count at least twenty vehicles. What brings them here?

I glance at Joel.

"Are they coming for Eddie?" I ask him. "Or for me? What did you tell your superiors?"

But perhaps I am too quick to judge, too harsh. Los Angeles has seen many strange sights lately, many bodies killed by superhumans. Perhaps Joel has not betrayed me, at least not intentionally. Perhaps I have betrayed myself. I have gotten sloppy in my old age. I hurry to Joel's side and shake him roughly.

"Wake up," I say. "We have to get out of here."

He opens his drowsy eyes. "You look different," he whispers.

"Your eyes are different."

Realization crosses his face. "Did you change me?"

"Yes."

He swallows weakly. "Am I still human?"

I sigh. "You're a vampire."

"Sita."

I put a finger to his lips. "Later. We must leave here quickly. Many cops are coming." I pull him to his feet and he groans. "You will feel stronger in a few minutes. Stronger than you have ever felt before."

I find a Bic lighter in the kitchen, and we head for

the front door. But before we can reach it I hear three cruisers skid to a halt outside. We hurry to the back, but the situation is the same. Cops, weapons drawn, have jumped out of their cars with whirling blue and red lights cutting paths in the night sky. More vehicles appear, armored monstrosities with SWAT teams inside. Searchlights flash on and light up the house. We are surrounded. I do not do well in such situations, or else, one might say, I do very well—for a vampire. What I mean is, being trapped brings out my most vicious side. I push aside my recently acquired revulsion for violence. Once, in the Middle Ages, surrounded by an angry mob, I killed over a hundred men and women.

Of course, they didn't have guns.

A bullet in the head could probably kill me, I think.

"Am I really a vampire?" Joel asks, still trying to catch up with reality.

"You're not an FBI agent anymore," I mutter.

He shakes himself as he straightens up. "But I am. Or at least they think I am. Let me talk to them."

"Wait." I stop him, thinking. "I can't have them examine Eddie's remains. I don't trust what will happen to his blood. I don't trust what his blood can still do. I must destroy it, and to do that I must burn down this house."

Outside, through a bullhorn, a gruff-voiced man calls for us to come out with our hands in the air. Such an unimaginative way of asking us to surrender.

Joel knew what Eddie had been capable of. "I was

wondering why everything smelled like gasoline," he remarks. "You light the place on fire—I have no problem with that. But then what are you going to do? You can't fight this army."

"Can't I?" I peer out the front window and raise my eyes to the rhythmic thrumming in the sky. They have a helicopter. Why? All to catch the feared serial killer? Yes, such a beast would demand heavy forces. Yet I sense a curious undercurrent in the assembled men and women. It reminds me of when Slim, Yaksha's assassin, came looking for me. Slim's people had been warned that I was not normal. As a result, I barely escaped. In the same way, these people know that there is something unusual about me.

I can almost read their thoughts.

This strikes me as strange.

I have always been able to sense emotions. Now, can I read thoughts, too?

What power has Yaksha's blood given me?

"Alisa," Joel says, calling me by my modern name. "Even you cannot break free of this circle." He notices I'm lost in thought. "Alisa?"

"They think there is a monster in here," I whisper. "I *hear* their minds." I grip Joel. "What did you tell them about me?"

He shakes his head. "Some things."

"Did you tell them I was powerful? Fast?"

He hesitates, then sighs. "I told them too much. But they don't know you're a vampire." He, too, peers through the curtains. "They were getting suspicious about how the others died, torn to pieces. They had my file on Eddie Fender, including where his mother lived. They must have tracked us here that way."

I shake my head. "I cannot surrender. It is against my nature."

He takes my hands. "You can't fight them all. You'll die."

I have to smile. "More of them would die." I lose my smile. "But if I do make a stand here, you will die also." I am indecisive. His advice is logical. Yet my heart betrays me. I feel doom closing in. I speak reluctantly. "Talk to them. Say what you think best. But I tell you—I will not leave this house without setting it ablaze. There will be no more Eddie Fenders."

"I understand." He turns for the door, then stops. He speaks with his back to me. "I understand why you did it."

"Do you forgive me?"

"Would I have died?" he asks.

"Yes."

He smiles gently, not turning to look at me. I feel the smile. "Then I must forgive you," he says. He raises his hands above his head and reaches for the doorknob. "I hope my boss is out there."

Through a crack in the curtains I follow his progress. Joel calls out his identity and a group of FBI agents step forward. I can tell they're FBI by their suits. Joel is one of them. He looks the same as he did yesterday. Yet they don't greet him as a friend. In an instant I grasp the full extent of their suspicions. They know that whatever plague of death has been sweeping L.A. is communicable. Eddie and I left too many bodies behind. Also, I remember the cop I freed. The one whose blood I sampled. The one I told I was a vampire. The authorities may not have believed that man, but they will think I am some kind of demon from hell.

Joel is handcuffed and dragged into an armored vehicle. He casts me a despairing glance before he vanishes. I curse the fact that I listened to him. Now I, too, must be taken into the vehicle. Above all, I must stay close to Joel. I don't know what he'll tell them. I don't know what they'll do with his blood.

Many of them are going to die, I realize.

The SWAT team cocks their weapons.

They call again for me to surrender.

I twirl the striker on the lighter and touch it to the wood I have gathered around Eddie's body. I say goodbye to his ugly head. Hope the Popsicles you suck in hell cool your cracked and bleeding lips. Casually, while the inferno spreads behind me, I step out the front door.

They are on me in an instant. Before I can reach the curb, my arms are pulled behind me and I am handcuffed. They don't even read me my rights. You have the right to a pint of blood. If you cannot afford one, the court will bleed a little for you. Yeah, I think sarcastically as they shove me into the back of the armored vehicle where they threw Joel, I will be given all my rights as an American citizen. Behind me I see them trying to put out the fire. Too bad they brought the firepower but forgot the fire engines. The house is a funeral pyre. Eddie Fender will leave no legacy to haunt mankind.

But what about me? Joel?

Our legs are chained to the floor of the vehicle. Three men with automatic weapons and ghostly faces lit from a single overhead light sit on a metal bench across from us, weapons trained on us. No one speaks. Another two armed men sit up front, beside the driver. One carries a shotgun, the other a machine gun. They are separated from us by what I know is bulletproof glass. It also acts as soundproofing. I can break it with my little finger.

But what about the miniature army around us? They won't break so easily. As the door is closed and we roll forward, I hear a dozen cars move into position around us. The chopper follows overhead, a spotlight aimed down on our car. Their precautions border on the fanatical. They know I am capable of extraordinary feats of strength. This realization sinks deep into my consciousness. For five thousand years, except for a few isolated incidents, I have moved unknown through human history. Now I am exposed. Now I am the enemy. No matter what happens, whether we escape or die trying, my life will never be the same.

I'll have to tear up my credit cards.

"Where are you taking us?" I ask.

"You are to remain silent," the middle one says. He has the face of a drill sergeant, leathery skin, deeply etched lines cut in from years of barking commands. Like his partners, he wears a flak jacket. I think I would look nice in one. I catch his eye and smile faintly.

"What's the matter?" I ask. "Are you afraid of a young woman?"

"Silence," he snaps, shaking his weapon, shifting uncomfortably. My stare is strong medicine. It can burn holes in brain neurons. My voice is hypnotic, when I wish it to be. I could sing a grizzly to sleep. I let my smile widen.

"May I have a cigarette?" I ask.

"No," he says flatly.

I lean forward as far as I can. These men, for all their plans, have not come as well prepared as Slim's people did. Yaksha had them bring cuffs made of a special alloy that I could not break. I can snap these like paper. Yet they are seated close together, these SWAT experts, and they have three separate weapons leveled directly at me. They could conceivably kill me before I could take out all of them. For that reason I have to take a subtle approach.

Relatively speaking.

"I don't know what you've been told about me," I continue. "But I think it's way out of line. I have done nothing wrong. Also, my friend here is an FBI agent. He shouldn't be treated this way. You should let him go." I stare deep into the man's eyes, and I know all he sees is my widening black pupils, growing as large as the dark sides of twin moons. I speak softly, "You should let him go *now.*"

The man reaches for his keys, then hesitates. The

hesitation is a problem. Pushing a person's will is always a hit-or-miss proposition. His partners are watching him now, afraid to look at me. The youngest one rises half off his bench. He is suddenly scared and threatens me with his weapon.

"You shut your goddamn mouth!" he yells.

I lean back and chuckle. As I do, I catch his eye. Fear has made him vulnerable; he is an easy mark. "What are you afraid of?" I ask. "That your commander will let me go? Or that you'll turn around and shoot him?" I bore my gaze into his head. "Yeah, you could shoot him. Yeah, that might be fun."

"Alisa," Joel whispers, not enjoying my game.

The young man and the commander exchange worried glances. The third guy has sat up, panting, not really understanding what is happening. Out of the corner of my eye, I see Joel shaking his head. Let him see me at my worst, I think. It is the best way to begin our new relationship, without illusions. My eyes dart from the commander to the young one. The temperature inside their craniums is increasing. Ever so slightly, each weapon begins to veer toward the other man's chest. Yet I know I'll have to push them a lot harder to get them to let me go or kill each other. It is not necessary. I can do it on my own. Really, I just want to distract them a bit—

Before I break them in two.

With their guns aimed away from me, they are vulnerable when I suddenly shoot my legs up, snapping my ankle chains. The third man, the one I have left untouched, reacts quickly, by human standards. But he is moving in slow motion compared to a five-thousand-year-old vampire. As he reaches for the trigger on his gun, my right foot lashes out and my big toe crushes his flak jacket, his breastbone, and the beating heart beneath the two. The heart beats no more. The man crumples and falls into a pitiful ball.

"Should have given me the cigarette," I say to the commander as I snap my handcuffs and reach over to take his head between my palms. His eyes grow round. His lips move. He wants to tell me something, maybe apologize. I'm not in the mood. He is putty in my hands, Silly Putty once I squeeze my palms together and crack his skull. Now his mouth falls open as his eyes slowly close. His brains leak out the back, over his starched collar. I don't want his flak jacket.

I glance over at the young one.

He's more scared than before.

I just stare at him. He has forgotten his weapon.

"Die," I whisper intently. My will is poisonous, when I am mad, and now, with Yaksha's blood in my veins, the poison is worse than the venom of a cobra. The young man falls to the floor.

His breathing stops.

Joel looks as if he will be sick.

"Kill me," he swears. "I cannot stand this."

"I am what I am." I break his chains. "You will become what I am."

He is bitter. He has no illusions. "Never."

I nod. "I said the same thing to Yaksha." I soften, touch his arm. "I cannot let them take you or me into custody. We could have a thousand Eddies running around."

"They just want to talk to us," he says.

I shake my head as I glance at the men up front, unaware, so far, of what has happened to their comrades. "They know we are not normal," I whisper.

Joel pleads. "You can escape far more easily without me. Fewer people will have to die. Leave me behind. Let them catch me in a shower of bullets. My blood will soak the pavement, nothing more."

"You are a brave man, Joel Drake."

He grimaces as he glances at what I have done to the others. "I have spent my life trying to help people. Not destroy them."

I stare softly into his eyes. "I can't just let you die. You don't know what I have sacrificed to keep you alive."

He pauses. "What did you sacrifice?"

I sigh. "The love of God." I turn toward the men at the front. "We will discuss this later."

Joel stops me one last time. "Don't kill when you don't have to."

"I will do what I can," I promise.

The bulletproof glass is two inches thick. Although the ceiling of the van forces me to crouch, I am able to leap far enough off the floor to plant two swift kicks onto the barrier. I have exceptionally strong legs. The glass shatters into thousands of little pellets. Before the two armed men can turn, I reach forward and knock their heads together. They collapse in a mangled heap. They are unconscious, not dead. I remove the revolver from the hip holster of the driver and place the barrel to his head.

"The men in the back are dead," I whisper in his ear. "If you glance in your rearview mirror you will see it is true. But I have allowed your partners up front to live. That is because I am a nice girl. I am nice and I am nasty. If you tell me where we are headed, I will be nice to you. If you don't, if you try to alert your partners on the road ahead of us or behind us, I will tear out your eyes and swallow them." I pause. "Where are you taking us?"

He has trouble speaking. "C-Fourteen."

"Is that a police station?"

"No."

"What is it? Quickly!"

He coughs, frightened. "A high-security facility."

"Who runs it?"

He swallows. "The government."

"Are there labs there?"

"I don't know. I've only heard stories. I think so."

"Interesting." I tap his head lightly with his gun. "What's your name?"

"Lenny Treber." He throws me a nervous glance. Sweat pours off him in a river. "What's your name?"

"I have many names, Lenny. We are in a tight fix here. You and I and my friend. How do we get out of it?"

He can't stop shaking. "I don't understand."

"I don't want to go to C-Fourteen. I want you to help me escape this dragnet. It is to your advantage to help, and to the advantage of your fellow cops. I don't want to leave several dozen women widowed." I pause. "Are you married, Lenny?"

He tries to calm himself with deep breaths. "Yes."

"Do you have children?"

"Yes."

"You don't want your children to grow up without a father, do you?"

"No."

"What can you do to help me and my friend?"

It is hard for him to concentrate. "I don't know."

"You will have to do better than that. What happens if you radio ahead and say you need to take a bathroom break?"

"They won't believe it. They'll know you have escaped."

"Is this van bulletproof?"

"Yes."

"What did they tell you about me?"

"That you were dangerous."

"Anything else?" I ask.

He is near tears. "They said you can kill with your bare hands." He catches a clear view of the brain tissue dripping out of the commander's skull. It is a gruesome sight, even by my flexible standards. A shudder runs through Lenny's body. "Oh God," he gasps.

I pat him sweetly on the back. "I do have my bad side," I admit. "But you cannot judge me by a few dead bodies. I don't want to kill you, Lenny, now that we're on a first-name basis. Think of another way for us to escape the escorts."

He struggles. "There isn't one. This job has the highest security imaginable. They'll open fire if I try to get away from them."

"Those were the orders?"

"Yes. Under no circumstances were you to be allowed to escape."

I ponder this. They must know me, even better than Lenny thinks. How's that possible? Have I left that much evidence behind? I think of the Coliseum, the necks I broke, the javelins I threw. It's possible, I suppose.

"I am going to escape," I tell Lenny, picking up the dropped machine gun and shotgun from the front seats. I also yank a flak jacket off one of the men. "One way or the other."

"They'll open fire," Lenny protests.

"Let them." I take ammunition for both weapons from the unconscious men. I gesture to Joel, who is still getting adjusted to his vampire senses. He's staring around the interior of the van as if he's stoned. "Put on one of those flak jackets," I tell him.

"Does there have to be shooting?" he asks.

"There will be a lot of shooting." I speak to Lenny. "What's the top speed of this van?"

"Eighty miles an hour."

I groan. "I need a cop car."

"There are a lot of them behind and in front of us," Lenny says.

I peer at the chopper in the sky. "They hang close to the ground."

"They're heavily armed," Lenny says. "They won't let you escape."

I climb in the front seat beside him, shoving the men aside. The flak jacket is a little large on me. "You think I should surrender?"

"Yes." He adds quickly, "That's just my opinion."

"You just follow my orders if you want to live," I say, studying the cruisers in front, in back. Sixteen altogether—two officers in each, I know. Plus there are at least three unmarked cars—FBI agents. It continues to amaze me how quickly they took Joel into custody. They hardly gave him a chance to speak. I call back to him, "Come up here. We're going to switch vehicles in a few minutes."

Joel pokes his head close to my shoulder, flak jacket in place. "The chopper is a problem," he says. "It doesn't matter how good a driver you are or how many cop cars you disable. It'll stay with us, lighting us up."

"Maybe. Put on a seat belt." I brace a foot on the dashboard and point to an approaching alley. "There, Lenny, I want you to take a hard left. Floor it as soon as you come out of the turn."

Lenny sweats. "OK."

I start to hand Joel Lenny's revolver. "Don't be afraid to cover my back." I pause and catch his eye. "You are on my side, aren't you?"

Joel hesitates. "I won't kill anybody."

"Will you try to kill me?"

"No."

I give him the revolver. "All right." The alley closes. "Get ready, Lenny. No tricks. Just put as much distance between us and the procession as you can."

Lenny veers to the left. The alley is narrow; the van shoots through it at high speed, knocking over garbage cans and crates. The response from the cops is immediate. Half the cars jam into the alley in pursuit. But half is better than all, and locked in behind us as they are, the cops can't fire at us so easily.

Unfortunately, the alley crosses several streets. Fortunately, it's midnight, with almost no traffic. At the first street we're lucky. But we lose two police cars to a collision. At the second crossing we're also fortunate. But as we drive into the third cross street we smash sideways into the only vehicle on the street, an open produce truck loaded with oranges. The fruit spills over the van. Lenny has bumped his head on the steering wheel and appears to be dazed. He gets another bump on his head when a squad car smashes into us from behind. This is what I wanted—a pileup.

"Come on!" I call to Joel.

I jump out of the side of the van and raise the machine gun and fire a spray of bullets at the cars piled up behind us. They are pinned down, but I know it won't be long before a herd of fresh cars comes around the block. The suddenness of my attack causes them to scramble from their vehicles. Overhead, the chopper swoops dangerously low, the spotlight mo-

18

mentarily focused straight on me. I look through the glare of the light and see a marksman stand in the open doorway and raise a high-powered rifle. Pumping the shotgun, I take aim at him and pull the trigger.

The man loses the top of his head.

His lifeless body falls onto the roof of a nearby building.

I am not finished.

My next shot takes out the spotlight. My third hits the small vertical rotor at the rear. The blade sputters but continues to spin. Pumping the shotgun, I put another round in it, and this time the propeller dies. It is the vertical rotor that prevents fuselage rotation and also provides rudder control. In other words, it gives stability to the helicopter. Immediately the flying machine veers out of control. To the horror of the watching police officers, it crash-lands in the midst of their line of cars. The explosion is violent, crushing several officers, setting a few ablaze. I use the distraction to reach in and pull Joel out of the van. We run down the block, faster than any human could.

All this has happened in ten seconds.

So far, not a single shot has been fired at us.

A second line of cop cars comes around the block.

I jump into the middle of the street and pour two shotgun rounds into the window of the first one, killing both officers inside. The vehicle loses control and crashes into a parked car. The police cars behind it slam on their brakes. A spray of bullets from my machine gun makes them scramble out of their vehicles in search of cover. I run toward the second car, shielding Joel with my body. To the police, I know, my movements appear as nothing more than a blur. They can't get a lock on me. Nevertheless, they do open fire and a hail of bullets flies around me. My flak jacket takes several rounds, causing no damage. But one bullet catches me in the leg above my left knee and I stumble, although I don't fall. Another shot hits me in my right upper arm. Somehow, I reach the second police car and shove Joel inside. I want to drive. I am bleeding, and the pain is intense, but I am in too much of a hurry to acknowledge it.

"Keep your head down!" I snap at Joel as I throw the car in gear. Peeling out, we are treated to another shower of bullets. I take my own advice and duck. Both the front and rear windshields shatter. Glass pellets litter my long blond hair. It will take a special brand of shampoo to get them out.

We escape, but are a marked couple in a highly visible car. I jump on the Harbor Freeway, heading north, hoping to put as much distance between us and our pursuers as quickly as possible. I keep the accelerator floored, weaving in and out of the few cars. But I have two police cars on my tail. Worse, another helicopter has appeared in the sky. This pilot has learned from his predecessor. He keeps the chopper up high, but not so high that he can't track us.

"We can't hide from a chopper," Joel says again.

"This is a big city," I reply. "There are many places to hide."

He sees I am bloody. "How bad are your injuries?"

It is an interesting question because already—in the space of a few minutes—they have completely healed. Yaksha's blood—it is an amazing potion.

"I am all right," I say. "Are you injured?"

"No." He pauses. "How many men have died since this started?"

"At least ten. Try not to count."

"Is that what you did after a few thousand years? You stopped counting?"

"I stopped thinking."

I have a goal. Because I know we cannot stay on the freeway long, I decide that the only way we can escape the helicopters is to get into one ourselves. Atop several of the high-rises in downtown Los Angeles there are helicopter pads with choppers waiting to whisk executives to high-level meetings. I can fly a helicopter. I can operate any piece of machinery humankind has developed.

I exit the freeway on Third Street. By now I have ten black-and-whites on my tail. Coming down the off ramp, I see several cop cars struggling to block the road in front of me. Switching to the wrong side of the street, I bypass them and head east in the direction of the tallest buildings. But my way is quickly blocked by another set of black-and-whites. We must have half the LAPD after us. I am forced to swerve into the basement garage of a building I don't know. A wooden bar swings down to block my way, but I don't stop to press the green button and collect my ticket. Nor does the herd of law enforcement behind me. We all barrel through the barricade. A sign for an elevator calls my attention and I slam the car to a halt inches from the door. We jump out and push the button. While we wait for our ride to higher floors, I open fire on our pursuers. More people die. I lied to Joel. I do count— three men and a woman take bullets in the face. I am a very good shot.

The elevator comes and we pile inside.

I press the top button. Number twenty-nine.

"Can they halt the elevator from the basement?" I ask as I reload.

"Yes. But it'll take them a few minutes to figure out how to do it." He shrugs. "But does it matter? They'll surround this building with an army. We're trapped."

"You're wrong," I say.

We exit onto the top floor. Here there are expensive suites, for law firms, plastic surgeons, and investment counselors. But there is too much high-priced real estate in Los Angeles—several of the suites are empty. Kicking in the door of the nearest vacancy, I stride up and down beside the wide windows, studying the neighboring buildings. I will have to cross the block and move over a few buildings to reach a high-rise that has a helicopter pad. I curse the fact that I am not a mythic vampire from films, capable of flying.

Yet I am able to leap tall buildings in a single bound.

Joel moves to my side. Below us, we watch the forces of righteousness gather. Two more helicopters have appeared in the night sky. Their bright beams rake the sides of the building.

"They won't come up the elevator after us," Joel says. "They will only come when they have us surrounded top and bottom." He pauses. "What are we going to do?"

"*I* am going to set a new Olympic record." I point to the building across the street. Its roof is only three stories below where we are. "I am going to jump over to it."

He is impressed. "That's far. Can you really do it?"

"If I get a running start. I'll come back for you in a few minutes, in a helicopter. I will land it on the roof of this building. Be waiting for me."

"What if you miss the roof of that building?"

I shrug. "It's a long way down."

"Could you survive the fall?"

"I think so. But it would take me time to recover."

"You shouldn't come back for me," Joel says. "Steal a helicopter and escape."

"That is not a consideration."

He speaks seriously. "Too many people have died. Even if we escape, I can't live with this slaughter on my conscience."

I am impatient. "Don't you see how dangerous you are to the human race? Even dead. They could take your blood, inject it into animals, into themselves— just as Eddie did. And they will do that, after witnessing what we can do. Believe me, I only kill tonight so that the world can wake safely in the morning."

"Is that true, Sita? You would die to save all these men and women?"

I turn away. "I would die to save you."

He speaks gently. "What did you sacrifice to keep me alive?"

I would weep, I think, if I could. "I told you."

"I didn't understand."

"It doesn't matter. It's done." I turn back to him. "There will be time later for these discussions."

He touches my hair—pieces of glass fall to the floor. "You miss him."

"Yes."

"I didn't know what he meant to you when I watched him die."

I smile sadly. "Nothing is really known about a person until he or she is gone."

"I cannot take his place."

I nod weakly. "I know." Then I shake my head. "I need to go."

He wants to hug me. "This could be goodbye."

"It is not over yet."

Before launching my daring leap, I kick out the window that blocks my way. This alerts the buzzing choppers but I don't give them time to zero in on me. I back away from the windows, taking only the shotgun with me, giving the machine gun to Joel.

"Are you afraid of heights?" he asks.

I kiss him. "You don't know me. I am afraid of nothing."

Taking a deep breath, I begin my hard approach. I

can accelerate sharply and be at full speed in less than ten strides. My balance and ability to judge distance are flawless. I hit the shattered bottom edge of the window perfectly and all at once I am airborne.

The flight across the gap between the buildings is breathtaking, even for me. It seems as if I'll float forever, moving horizontally, in defiance of gravity. The searchlights on the helicopters are too slow to catch me. I soar in darkness, a huge bat, the cool air on my face. Below, the tiny figures raise their heads skyward, blinking at the impossible. I almost laugh. They thought they had me trapped, silly mortals. They thought wrong.

My landing is not entirely smooth because I have such momentum. I am forced into a roll as I skitter across the rooftop. I am bleeding as I finally come to a halt and jump up. Overhead the choppers are frantically maneuvering to open fire. I am not given a chance to catch my breath before moving. Leaping for the next rooftop, I watch as a line of bullets rips a path in front of me.

The ensuing jumps between buildings are all on the same side of the street and not so dramatic as the first one. Yet the last leap, to the skyscraper with the helicopter pad, is to be the most dramatic of all. Because I cannot jump to the top of a building twenty stories up, I do not plan to land on top of the skyscraper. I will jump *into* it, through its wall of windows. I only hope that I don't hit the steel and concrete between floors.

Once again, the choppers approach, their machine guns blasting.

Once again, I take a running start.

The windows of the skyscraper rush toward me like a hard black wall. An instant before contact, I lean back and kick out with my feet. My timing is perfect; the glass shatters around the lower part of my body, sparing my face and arms. Unfortunately, I land awkwardly on a row of secretarial desks. The shock is incredible, even for me. Coming to a halt in a pile of ruined PCs and paper clips, I lie still for a whole minute, trying to catch my breath. I am now covered with blood from head to toe. Yet even as I grimace in pain my flesh wounds begin to close and my broken bones begin to mend.

I have company on the outside. One of the helicopter pilots has taken it upon himself to come level with the hole I have punched into the side of the skyscraper. The chopper floats just outside the shattered window, scanning the office with its bright searchlight. There are three men, including the pilot, aboard the craft. Peering through the wreckage, I notice that the machine gunner has an itchy finger. I think to myself how much more I would prefer to have a police chopper than a civilian one. But the pilot is not reckless. He keeps the chopper constantly moving a little from side to side. For me to try to leap onto it would be risky. I opt for the more conservative plan.

I get up slowly, limping. My right shinbone is still fractured, but it will be all right in another minute—

God bless Yaksha's blood. Ducking behind the desks, the beam from the searchlight stretching long, stark shadows across the office, I move away from the broken window. The helicopter swoops in a narrow arc, sometimes onto the far side of the hole, sometimes closer to where I'm hidden. The windows are tinted; it is easier for me to follow their movements than for them to follow mine, unless their light were to hit me directly. Yet they seem obsessed with the space just beyond the hole. They must feel that I am in the wreckage somewhere near it, injured and dying.

"Come to me baby," I whisper.

On their third swing toward my side, I punch out the window in front of me and open fire. I take out the machine gunner first; I don't like his looks. The searchlight goes next. I take aim on the fuel tank. As I said, I enjoy fireworks, wicked explosions. When I pull the trigger on the shotgun, the chopper detonates in a huge fireball. The pilot screams, the flames engulfing his body. The other man is blown out the side door, in pieces. The life goes out of the machine and it sinks to the ground. Far below I hear people crying. Far above, to my right, I hear the other two helicopters veer away. They have lost enthusiasm for the fight.

On the way to the elevator, I pass a custodian. He hardly looks up. Despite my blood and artillery, he wishes me a good evening. I smile at him.

"You have a good night," I say.

The elevator takes me to the top floor, and from

there it is not hard to find a private access ladder onto the roof. Not one but two helicopters wait to fly us to freedom. Both are jet powered and I am pleased. They will at least be as fast as the cops' choppers, if not faster. Unfortunately there's a security guard on duty. An old guy, obviously working the night shift to supplement a meager retirement, he takes one look at me and hurries over. He has a handgun but doesn't draw it. His glasses are remarkably thick; he squints through the lenses as he looks me up and down.

"Are you a cop?" he asks.

I don't have the heart to lie to him. "No. I'm the bad guy. I'm the one who just blew that chopper out of the sky."

He is awestruck. "I watched you jumping from building to building. How do you do that?"

"Steroids."

He slaps his leg. "I knew it! The drugs young people are taking these days. What do you want? One of these choppers?"

I point my shotgun at him. "Yes. Please give me the keys. I don't want to have to kill you."

He quickly raises his hands. "You don't have to do that. The keys are in the ignitions. Do you know how to fly a helicopter?"

I turn my weapon aside. "Yes. I've been taking lessons. Don't worry about me."

He walks me to the closest chopper, a Bell 230. "This baby has a range of over three hundred miles. You want to get far out of town. The radio and TV are babbling about you, calling you a band of Arab terrorists."

I laugh as I climb into the cockpit. "You do nothing to destroy their illusions. Just tell them you were overwhelmed by superior forces. You don't want people to know a young woman stole a helicopter out from under your nose."

"And a blond one at that," he agrees. "You take care!"

He closes the door for me and I'm off.

Picking up Joel proves to be the easiest part of the night. The police helicopters are holding back—over a mile away. They aren't used to being blown out of the sky. The fire from the last downed chopper spreads over the front of the skyscraper. In the distance I see smoke from the first chopper. Joel shakes his head as he climbs in.

"They'll never stop hunting us after this," he says.

"I don't know," I jest. "They might be afraid to come after me."

We head northeast. I'm anxious to get out of the suburban sprawl and into the wild, somewhere we can disappear. The nearby mountains are a possibility. Our chopper is fast, capable of going two hundred miles an hour. To my surprise, the police helicopters don't really pursue us. It's not just because we're faster than they are—a fact I have to question. They allow the gap to grow between us to at least twenty miles. The length of the space doesn't reassure me because I know they still have us under visual observation.

Nothing will be gained by plunging low to the ground below the radar. They are waiting for something biding their time.

"Reinforcements," I mutter as we swoop over the sleeping city at an elevation of a thousand feet.

Joel nods. "They've called for bigger guns."

"Army helicopters?"

"Probably."

"Which direction will they come from?"

"There is a large base south of here. You might want to head north."

"I was planning to do so after I reached the Cajon Pass." The pass cuts into the desert, also a nice place to hide. Highway 15 runs through the pass, and if followed far enough, leads to Las Vegas.

"You might not want to wait that long," Joel advises.

"I understand." Yet the temptation to put more distance between us and our pursuers is great. It gives me the illusion of safety, a dangerous illusion. But the farther we go, the more the desert beckons me. Being winter, the mountains are covered with snow, and even though I am highly resistant to cold, I don't like it. At our present speed Cajon Pass is not far ahead. Once over it, we will be clear of the city, able to roam free.

I ask the question I have been waiting to ask.

"Are you thirsty?"

He is guarded. "What do you mean?"

I glance over. "How do you feel?"

He takes a deep breath. "Feverish. Cramping."

I nod. "You need blood."

He takes time to absorb my words. "Do you really drink people's blood? Like in the stories?"

"The stories have germs of truth in them, but can't be taken literally. As a vampire, you do need blood to survive. Yet you do not need to kill the person you drink from, and your contact with them will not change them into vampires. You can also live off the blood of animals, although you will find it unsatisfying."

"Do I need blood every day?"

"No. Every few days. But at first, you will crave it every day."

"What happens if I don't drink it?"

"You will die horribly," I say.

"Oh. Do I still need to eat regular food?"

"Yes. You will get hungry as before. But if need be, you will be able to survive for a long time without food. You will also be able to hold your breath for incredible lengths of time."

"But what about the sun? You sat out in the sun with me."

"Yes. But that is not something you want to try yet. The sun won't kill you, but it will irritate you, at least for the first few centuries. Even now, after five thousand years, I'm not nearly so strong while the sun is up. But forget everything else you've heard about vampires. Crucifixes and white roses and running water—none of those will bother you. Bram Stoker was just spicing up his novel when he wrote that stuff." I pause. "Did you know I met him once?"

"Did you tell him you were a vampire?"

"No, but he knew there was something special about me. He autographed my copy of *Dracula* and tried to get my address. But I didn't give it to him." I raise my wrist to my mouth. "I am going to open my vein. I want you to suck my blood for a few minutes."

He fidgets. "Sounds kinky."

"You'll enjoy it. I taste wonderful."

A moment later Joel reluctantly accepts my bleeding wrist, but he is no Ray. He has seen plenty of blood in his line of work and it doesn't make him sick to his stomach. Indeed, after a couple of minutes he is sucking hungrily on my wrist. I have to stop him before he is sated. I cannot allow my strength to wane.

"How do you feel?" I ask as I take back my arm.

"Powerful. Aroused."

I have to laugh. "Not every girl you meet will be able to do that for you."

"Can we be killed with a stake through the heart?"

The laughter dies in my throat. His question brings back the agony of the wound I suffered when my house exploded and Yaksha supposedly died. The chest pain is still there—yet, since drinking Yaksha's blood, it has receded. I wonder what Yaksha would think of me now that I have broken Krishna's vow against creating more vampires. After I have killed so many innocent people. No doubt he would say I am damned.

I miss Yaksha. And Ray. And Krishna.

"You can be killed that way," I say quietly.

Ten minutes later we reach the gap in the mountains

and I veer north, climbing in altitude. The pass is almost a mile above sea level. The police helicopters are now thirty miles behind us, blinking red and white dots in the night sky. We have at most four hours of night left. Before then, I must find shelter for Joel and a place to sit quietly and plot my next moves. Scanning left and right, I consider dumping the helicopter. The cliffs of the pass offer more hiding places than the desert will. Yet I don't want to set down so soon. Another idea has come to me, one that may throw our pursuers off.

What if I were to crash the helicopter into a lake?

It would sink and hopefully leave no sign behind.

The plan is a good one. Fuel dictates I choose the closest lake, Big Bear or Arrowhead. But once again I resist heading into the snowy mountains. As a newborn, Joel will not fare well there. I remember how sensitive I was to the cold after Yaksha changed me. Vampires, serpents, the offspring of yakshinis—we prefer warmth.

I need a sand dune oasis with a lake in the center of it.

We plunge over the pass and into the desert.

The bleak landscape sweeps beneath us.

Time passes. I cannot see anyone following.

"We can't stay up here forever," Joel says finally.

"I know."

"What are you waiting for?"

"Lake Mead." Hoover Dam—it is only twenty minutes away, I estimate.

But I have waited too long.

Five minutes later I catch sight of two military helicopters, coming at us from the west, not the south. Because my eyes are so sharp, I see them far off—sixty miles away. I feel it is still possible to reach the lake. Yet I know they have spotted us, that they are tracking us on their radar. When I alter course slightly, they do likewise. Joel sees my concern but doesn't understand it at first. Even changed, his sight is no match for mine.

"What is it?" he asks.

"We have company," I say.

He looks around. "Can we reach the lake?"

"Possibly." I ask in jest, "Can we fight two Apache helicopters?"

"No way."

I guess at the type of craft that pursues us, but a few minutes later I see that I was right. My knowledge of the Apache isn't extensive, but I have read enough to know that we are facing the most lethal attack helicopter on earth. The two choppers move close to each other, on a direct intercept course with us. Black as the desert sky, with wide hypnotic propellers—they are clearly faster than we are. Their machine-gun turret and rocket launchers hang from the sides like dangerous fists. They sweep toward us for a knockout punch. Joel sees them.

"Maybe we should surrender," he suggests.

"I never surrender."

They catch us three miles short of the lake. The

wide flat expanse of water is clearly visible, but it could be on the other side of the moon for all the good it can do us now. That's what I think at first. Yet the Apaches do not immediately lock on their weapons. They swoop above and below us, dangerously close, ordering us to land.

"Somebody has told them to take us alive," Joel observes.

"Who?"

Joel shrugs. "The order could have come from the President of the United States. But I suspect the commander of the base where these helicopters originated has given the order."

"We only need to get to the water," I say. "They couldn't imagine that we'd try to vanish underwater."

"I can't imagine it. Can we really hold our breath a long time?"

"I can go an hour."

"But what about me?"

I pat his leg. "Have faith. We should have died a dozen times tonight and we're still alive. Maybe Krishna hasn't deserted us after all."

"If they open fire in the next minute we might have a chance to ask him directly," Joel says dryly.

The Apaches buzz us a couple of times more, then grow tired of the cat-and-mouse game. They lay down a stream of bullets across our path and I have to slow sharply to avoid being torn to shreds. Still, they could blow us out of the sky whenever they wish. Yet they hold back, although they don't want me flying above the lake. They try blocking our path and I have to go into a steep dive to stay on course. We come within several feet of the ground and Joel almost has a heart attack.

"You are one mean pilot," he says when he catches his breath.

"I'm pretty good in bed as well," I reply.

"Of that I have no doubt."

These military men are not like the LAPD. They expect their orders to be obeyed. They may have instructions to take us alive, but they also have orders to prevent us from escaping. A quarter mile from the water, they open fire with surgical precision and suddenly our rotor blades are not a hundred percent intact. Our copter falters in the air, but stays up. The noise above us is deafening. Yet I continue on toward the lake. I have no choice.

"Get ready to jump," I tell Joel.

"I'm not leaving till you leave."

"Nice line. But you have to jump as soon as we cross over the water. Swim for the far shore, not the near one. Stay under water as long as possible."

Joel hesitates. "I don't know how to swim."

"What?"

"I said I don't know how to swim."

I can't believe it. "Why didn't you tell me that earlier?"

"I didn't know what you had planned. You didn't tell me."

"Joel!"

"Sita!"

I pound the chopper dashboard. "Damn! Damn! Well, you're just going to have to learn how to swim. You're a vampire. All vampires can swim."

"Says who?"

"Says me, and I'm the only authority on the subject. Now stop arguing with me and prepare to jump."

"You jump with me."

"No. I have to wait until they fire their lethal blow—that way they'll think I'm dead."

"That's crazy. You will be dead."

"Shut up and crack your door slightly. When you reach the far shore, run into the hills and hide. I'll find you. I can hear a vampire breathing ten miles away."

The Apaches are still determined to prevent us from reaching the water. One swoops overhead and literally drops itself directly into our path. I have to go into another steep dive to avoid it, which is easy to do because the craft is ready to crash anyway. The water is now only a hundred yards away. The Apache behind us opens fire. They mimic my earlier strategy. They blow off our tail rotor. I immediately lose control. We spin madly to the left. Yet the water is suddenly below us.

"Jump!" I scream at Joel.

He casts me one last glance—his expression curiously sad.

Then he is gone.

Pulling back hard on the steering bar, I try to gain altitude, partly to distract them from Joel and partly to stay alive. It is my hope they didn't see him jump. My chopper swings farther out over the water. A mile away I see Hoover Dam. There is no way I can make it that far. The chopper bucks like a hyperactive horse on speed. Cracking my door, I take hold of the shotgun and blast at one of the Apaches as it swings nearby. I hit the top blades, but these suckers are tough. The military chopper banks sharply. Then the two helicopters regroup, hovering behind me, twin hornets studying a wounded butterfly. Over my shoulder I see one pilot nod to his gunner. The man reaches for a fresh set of controls, no doubt the firing mechanism for the rockets. As I throw my door open wide, an orange tongue of flame leaps out from the side of the Apache. My reflexes are fast, blinding by human standards, but even I cannot outrun a missile. I am barely free of my seat when the rocket hits.

My chopper vaporizes in midair.

The shock from the explosion hits with the power of an iron fist. A fragment of burning metal cuts into my skull above my hairline, sending waves of searing pain through my whole system. I topple like a helicopter without a stabilizing propeller. Blood pours over my face and I am blinded. I do not see the cold water of the lake approaching, but I feel it when it slaps my broken side. The molten shrapnel in my head shudders as it contacts the dark liquid. A burst of steam almost causes my skull to explode. I feel myself spiraling down into a forsaken abyss. Consciousness flickers in and out. The lake is bottomless, my soul as empty as dice without numbers. As I start to black out, I wish that I didn't have to die this way—without Krishna's grace. How I would love to see him on the other side—his divine blue eyes. God forgive me, how I love him.

2

I awake with a pale wash of light panning across my face. Opening my eyes, I see it is the searchlights of hovering helicopters pointing down on me. Only they are high in the air, and I am many feet underwater, on my back, on the bottom of the lake. Even though unconscious, my mind must have had the wisdom to halt my breathing. I don't know how long I have been out. My head still hurts but the pain is bearable. It is obvious that the personnel in the helicopters cannot see me.

I wonder how Joel is, if he escaped.

My left leg is pinned under the wreckage of my chopper. It is good because otherwise I would be floating on the surface, probably with many bullet holes in me. Pulling my leg free, I roll over on my belly and begin to swim away from the lights, not sure at first if I am moving deeper into the lake or closer to the shore. My desire for breath is strong but not overwhelming. I know I can swim a long way before I'll have to surface. They can't scan every square inch of the lake. I am going to escape.

Yet there will be no freedom for me if Joel is not free.

Ten minutes later, when the lights are far behind me, I allow myself to swim to the surface and peek. I am far out in the center of the lake. Behind me, near the shore where my chopper was blown out of the sky, the helicopters still circle, their beams still focused on the water. Close to this spot, on the shore, are several trucks, many uniformed people, some cops, some army personnel. Joel stands in the middle of them, a dozen guns pointed at his head.

"Damn," I whisper. "He really couldn't swim."

I cannot rush in to save him. I know this yet I have to stop myself from making the attempt. It is my nature to act quickly. Patience has not come to me over the centuries. Floating in the center of the black lake, it seems to me the years have only brought grief.

Joel is ushered into an armored truck. Men on the shore are donning scuba gear. They want my body, they want to see it before they can rest. I know that I must act quickly if I am to track Joel. Yet I also know I have to stop killing. They'll be looking for any suspicious deaths in the area as a way to confirm I am still alive. A throbbing sensation in my forehead draws my attention. I reach up and pull away a chunk of shrapnel that has been working its way out of my skull. Before the infusion of Yaksha's blood, such an injury would have killed me.

I swim for the shore where Joel is being held, but a mile to the left, away from him and the dam. I am a better swimmer than most dolphins and reach land in a few minutes. No one sees me as I slip out of the water and dash into the rocky hills. My first impulse is to creep closer to the armed assembly. Yet I cannot steal one of their vehicles to follow Joel. Fretting about the growing gap between us, I turn away from the small army and run toward the campgrounds. Even in the winter, families come to Lake Mead to enjoy the nature. Overhead, an almost full moon shines down on me. Just what I don't need. If an Apache spots me again, I swear, I am going to jump up and grab its skids and take it over. My turn to fire the rockets.

The thoughts are idle, the mental chatter of a natural born predator.

I find a family of three asleep in a tent on the outskirts of the campground, their shiny new Ford Bronco parked nearby and waiting for me to steal. Silently, I break the lock and slip in behind the steering wheel. It takes me all of two seconds to hot-wire the vehicle. Then I am off, the window down.

Throughout my long life, hearing has always been my best sense. I can hear snowflakes as they emerge from a cloud two miles overhead. Indeed, I have no trouble hearing the army's motor parade start their engines and pull away from the lake. Probably the commander thinks he should get Joel to a secure place, even before the body of the blond witch is found. I use my ears to follow them as they move onto a road that leads away from the lake. Yet, with my nose in the air, it is my sense of smell that is the most acute. It startles me. I can smell Joel—even in the midst of the others—clearly, in fact. I suspect this is another gift of Yaksha, master yakshini, born of a demonic race of serpents. Snakes always have exceptional senses of smell.

I am grateful for this newfound sense because I can accurately trail the military parade from a great distance. These people are not stupid—they will check to see if they are being followed. Once again I am struck by my ability to sense their thoughts. I have always been able to discern emotions in mortals, but never ideas. Yaksha must have been an outright mind reader. He never told me. I know for sure the people up ahead are checking their backs. I allow the distance between us to grow to as much as fifteen miles. Naturally I drive with the lights out.

At first the group heads in the direction of Las Vegas. Then, five miles outside the City of Sin, they turn east onto a narrow paved road. The column stretches out and I have to stay even farther back. There are many signs: RESTRICTED AREA. I believe we are headed to some sort of government base.

My hunch is confirmed less than an hour later. Approximately fifty miles outside of Las Vegas, the armored vehicle carrying Joel disappears into an elaborately defended camp. I speed up and take my

Bronco off the road, parking it behind a hill a mile from both the road and the camp. On foot, I scamper toward the installation, growing more amazed with every step at how complex and impenetrable it appears. The surrounding fence is over a hundred feet high, topped with billowy coils of barbed wire. Ordinarily I could jump such a barrier without breaking a sweat. Unfortunately, the place has manned towers equipped with machine guns and grenade launchers every two hundred feet. That's a lot of towers. The compound is huge, at least a half mile across. In addition to the towers and fence, there is a densely packed maze of three-foot high electronic devices—they resemble metal baseball bats—stretched along the perimeter. I suspect that if tripped they emit a paralyzing field. Vampires are sensitive to electricity. I was once hit by a bolt of lightning and spent the next three days recovering in a coffin. My boyfriend at the time wanted to bury me.

One side of the compound is devoted almost exclusively to a concrete runway. I remember reading about a top-secret government installation in the desert outside of Las Vegas that supposedly tests advanced fighter craft, nuclear weapons, and biological weapons. I have a sneaking suspicion that I am looking at it. The compound backs into a large barren hill, and I believe the military has mined deep into the natural slope to perform experiments best hidden from the eyes of spy satellites.

There are Sherman tanks and Apache helicopters parked close to barracklike structures. No doubt the weapons can be manned in ten seconds. One thing is immediately clear to me.

I will not be able to break into the compound.

Not and get out alive.

The armored vehicle carrying Joel has halted near the center of the compound. Armed soldiers scurry to line up around it, their weapons drawn and leveled. A cruel-faced general with a single star on his shoulder and death in his eyes approaches the vehicle. Behind him is a group of white-clad scientists—just what I don't want to see. The general signals to somebody out of view and the side door on the armored vehicle swings open. Heavily chained, his shoulders bowed down, Joel is brought into the open. The general approaches him, strangely unafraid, and searches him. Then he glances over his shoulder. Several of the scientists seem to nod. I don't understand the exchange. What are they approving? That Joel is a genuine vampire? They don't know about vampires.

"Or do they?" I whisper.

But it's not possible. For the last two thousand years or more, Yaksha and I were the only vampires on earth. Recently there have been others, of course. But Ray's conversion was short-lived, Eddie was a psychotic aberration, and I destroyed all of Eddie's offspring.

Or did I?

This general wanted us taken alive, I realize. He's the one who gave the order to the Apache pilots. They waited a long time before they used their rockets, and then only when they were forced to. In fact, the general is probably angry that they used them at all. The way he's studying Joel—it's almost as if he's gloating. The general wants something from Joel, and he knows what it is.

Joel is taken inside a building.

The general confers with one scientist and then they, too, go inside.

I sit back and groan. "Damn."

My objective is clear. I have to get Joel out of the compound before they can perform extensive tests on him—more specifically, before they can analyze his blood. I'm not even sure what they will find, but whatever they discover, it won't bode well for the long-term survival of the human race.

But I cannot force my way inside. Therefore, I must sneak in. How do I do that? Make friends with the guards? Seduce Mr. Machine Gun Mike? The idea may not be as farfetched as it seems with my magnetic personality and hypnotic eyes. But from what I can see, all the men live at the compound. This is unfortunate.

I glance in the direction of Las Vegas, neon fallout on the horizon.

"But the boys must leave the compound and go out on the town now and then," I mutter.

It is two hours before dawn. While I study the compound with my powerful eyes, searching for a vulnerable spot, I see the scientist whom the general conferred with climb into an ordinary car. He stops at a checkpoint before exiting the compound. By then I am running for my Bronco.

I want to talk to this scientist.

46

As I climb in my stolen vehicle, I notice that my arms and hands are glowing with a faint white light. The effect stuns me. My face is also glowing! In fact, all my exposed skin shines with the same iridescence as the full moon, which hangs low in the sky in the direction of Las Vegas.

"What kind of radiation are they fooling with out here?" I mutter.

I decide to worry about it later.

The scientist is a speed demon. He drives close to a hundred all the way to Las Vegas, or at least until he hits the public highway, five miles outside the town. I push the Bronco to keep up. I suppose no cop will give him a ticket on a government road. It is my hope he lives in Vegas, but when he goes straight to the Mirage Hotel, my hopes sink. He's probably just out for a few hours of fun.

I park near him in the lot and prepare to follow him inside.

Then I remember what I am wearing.

A ripped flak jacket and bloody clothes.

I do not panic. The people I stole the Bronco from are on vacation. They will have, I'm sure, ladies' clothes somewhere in the vehicle. Lo and behold, in the back I find a pair of blue jeans, two sizes too big, and a black Mickey Mouse sweatshirt that fits like a wet suit. Luckily, the blood and glass washed out of my hair while I slept beneath Lake Mead. Standing in a dark corner of the parking lot, I change quickly.

I find the scientist inside at the dice table.

He is an attractive man, perhaps forty-five, with thick black hair and large sensual lips. His face is sun dried, tanned and lined, yet on him the effect is not unpleasant. He looks like a man who has weathered many storms and come out ahead. His gray eyes are deep set, very alert, focused. He has discarded his white lab coat for a nicely tailored sports coat. He is holding a pair of red dice as I enter, and it seems to me that he is secretly willing them to obey his commands, as so many other gamblers do.

He fails to throw a pass, a seven, or an eleven. He loses his bet and the dice pass to another player. I note that he had a hundred-dollar chip on the table, not a small bet for a scientist on the government payroll. I am surprised when he lays down another hundred dollars. He loses that as well.

I observe the man for forty-five minutes. He is a regular—one of the pit bosses calls him Mr. Kane, another, Andy. Andrew Kane, I think. Because Andy continues to lose, at an alarming rate, he is forced to sign a slip to get more chips when the cash in his pockets is gone. But these black honeybees vanish rapidly, and his eagerness turns to frustration. I have been counting. Two thousand dollars gone—just like that. Sighing, he leaves the table and, after a double scotch at the bar, leaves the casino.

I follow him home. The place is modest.

He goes inside and prepares for bed. As the morning sun splashes the eastern sky, he turns out his own light. Obviously he works the night shift. Or else the general had called Andy into work because of Joel. I wonder if he will be working long hours in the days to come. Memorizing his address, I drive back toward the Mirage. If it is Andy's favorite hangout, it'll be mine as well.

I have no credit cards, money, or identification, but the woman at the reservation desk hands me a key to a luxury suite after staring hard into my beautiful blue eyes. Inside my room, I place a call to my primary business manager in New York City. His voice is unaffected—the government has not gotten to him yet. We do not talk long.

"Code red," I say. "Have the package delivered to the Mirage Hotel, Las Vegas. Room Two-One-Three-Four. Immediately."

"Understood," he says and hangs up.

The package will include everything I need to start a new life: passport, driver's license, cash, and credit cards. It will arrive at my door in the next hour. There will also be an elaborate makeup kit inside, wigs and different-colored contacts. Over the last fifty centuries, I have prepared for every eventuality, including this one. Tomorrow I will look like someone else, and Andrew Kane will meet a mysterious young woman, and fall in love.

3

The following evening a demure redhead with short bangs and green eyes waits outside Andrew Kane's house. Actually, I have been in the front seat of my newly purchased Jeep since noon, but the mad scientist has been fast asleep, as most normal people would be after staying up all night. I came to his house early because I am anxious to go through his things, learn exactly what he does before I make a move on him. The one fact that guides me as to his importance is that the general spoke only to him after Joel was brought inside the compound. Yet intuitively I sense Andy's value. There is something fascinating in his gray eyes, even though he is a degenerate gambler. This quality does not bother me, however, because I might be able to use his obvious casino debt against him. Of course, I plan to use Andy to get into the compound to rescue Joel.

Quickly. I feel the pressure of each passing hour.

Joel will be thirsty already, unless they happen to feed him.

A newborn's thirst is agonizing.

The papers are shouting about the barbaric terrorist attack in Los Angeles. Authorities estimate that there were at least three dozen Islamic fanatics involved, and that the local police were overwhelmed by superior forces and military equipment. The mayor has vowed that the city officials will not rest until the murderers are brought to justice.

When in doubt, blame it on the Arabs.

The hot sun is draining for me after such an intense night. Yet I bear it better than I would have before drinking Yaksha's blood. I suspect, after five thousand years, the sun had no effect on Yaksha. I sure could use his power now. I pray he is finally at peace, in Krishna's blue abode. How often I pray to Krishna. How curious, since I am supposed to hate him. Oh well, the heart of a vampire is unfathomable. No wonder superstitious people are always trying to drive stakes through our hearts.

It is five in the evening before Andrew Kane emerges from his house and climbs in his car. He has no time for the casinos now. No doubt the general waits for him. Andy drives the five miles on Highway

15, then turns onto the government road, once again pushing his speed up to near a hundred. My Jeep has a powerful engine—I cruise five comfortable miles behind him. Actually, it is probably something of a waste to follow him all the way into work. He'll just drive inside and disappear into one of the buildings. But I want to see how long it takes him to pass through security, how many checks he goes through. Close to the compound, I veer off the road and tear across the desert, parking near the hill I hid behind before. On the seat beside me are high-powered binoculars. Even my supernatural sight can be improved by mechanical aids.

I am not given a chance to reach my vantage point before Andy gets to the front gate of the compound. Still, I can see well enough. He is stopped, naturally, but the guards know him well. He hardly has to flash his badge. The guards do not search his trunk. He parks his car in the same spot and enters the building where Joel was taken, the largest, most modern building in the whole complex. Chemical smells drift out from the building. It definitely has a lab inside.

I would like to examine the compound further but night is the time to do it. Plus I am anxious to get into Andy's house. I tear back to Las Vegas, not passing anyone on the road. I wonder if the scuba divers are still searching the bottom of Lake Mead for my body. I wonder if the general suspects I will try to rescue Joel. I doubt it.

Andy's house is a three-bedroom affair at the end of a quiet cul-de-sac. This being Las Vegas, there is the obligatory pool in the backyard. Leaving my Jeep on the adjoining street, I climb his wall and pick his back door lock. Inside it is cool; he left the air conditioning on. I shut the door and stand listening for a moment, smelling. Many aromas come to me then. They tell me much about the man, even though we have never been formally introduced.

He is a vegetarian. There is no smell of animal flesh. He doesn't smoke, but he does drink. I see as well as smell the bottles of liquor in a walnut cabinet. He does not use cologne, but there is a faint odor of various makeup products. Our Mr. Andrew Kane resents middle age.

He is a bachelor, there are no pictures of a wife or kids on the walls. I step into the kitchen. He eats out mostly; there is little food in the refrigerator. I riffle through his bills on the kitchen counter. There are a couple of envelopes from banks. He is up to his limit on three credit cards.

I walk into the bedroom he uses as an office.

I almost faint.

On his desk is a black and white and red plastic model of the double helix DNA molecule. That is not what staggers me. Beside it is a much more complex model of a different kind of DNA—one that has twelve strands of encoded information instead of two. It is not the first time I have seen it. Seven hundred years ago, the great Italian alchemist, Arturo Evola, created a similar model after spending six months in my company.

"It's not possible," I whisper.

Andrew Kane has already begun to crack the DNA of the vampire.

4

Italy, during the thirteenth century, embodied all that was wonderful and horrible about the Middle Ages. The Catholic Church was the supreme power. Monarchs came and went. Kings and queens fought and died. But the Roman Pope wielded the true power over life and death.

Art was the gift of the Church to the people in those days. This was above and beyond the gift of their strict theology, which did nothing for the poor masses except keep them confused until the day they died. I say that with well-deserved bitterness. It would have been impossible to live in those days and not become angry at the Church. Today, however, I think the Church does much that is good, and much that is questionable. No religion is perfect, not after man gets through with it.

I lived in Florence from 1212 till 1245 and spent many months touring the churches where the finest paintings and sculptures were displayed. The Renaissance was, of course, a long way off, and Michelangelo and Da Vinci had yet to be born. Still, these earlier days were remarkable for their creativity. I remember well Bonaventura Berlinghieri's radiant *St. Francis* and Niccola Pisano's hypnotic sculpture *Annunciation to the Shepherds*.

The Inquisition was another gift of the Church. The boon of the devil in the minds of most people in those days. Two informants, whose identities could remain unknown to the victim, were all that was necessary to charge someone with being a heretic. The informants could be heretics themselves, or witches—not pleasant titles to earn in old Italy. A confession was necessary to convict anyone of being a heretic. A little stretching of the limbs, or burning with live coals, or torturing the victim on the *strappado*—the dreaded vertical rack—was usually enough to get an innocent person to confess. I remember going to the central city courtyard to watch the victims being burned alive at the stake. I used to think back over the barbarism of the Emperors of the Roman Empire, the Mongolian hordes, the Japanese shoguns—and yet their forms of torture all paled compared to the pain caused by the Church because the people who lit the pyres wore crosses. They chanted prayers while their victims screamed and died.

I observed only a few executions before I lost the stomach for them. Yet I thwarted the Inquisition in my own way, by secretly killing many of the inquisitors. I usually left their bodies in compromised places —houses of prostitution and the like—to discourage thorough investigations. As I drained the inquisitors' blood, sucking their large neck veins and arteries, I whispered in their ears that I was an angel of mercy. None of them died easily.

Yet the Church was bigger than a single vampire, the Inquisition an infection that spread and multiplied through its own mysterious madness. It could not be easily stopped. It cast a gloom over my stay in Florence, over my joy in the resurgence of mankind's creativity. I have hunted humans throughout time, and yet I am proud of them as well, when they do something bold, something unexpected. The best art always comes unbidden.

Arturo Evola was not known as an alchemist or else he would not have lasted a day in medieval Florence. He was a twenty-one-year-old Franciscan priest, and a devout one at that. He had entered the priesthood at the age of sixteen, which was not unusual at that time, because the easiest way to obtain the finest education was to become a priest. He was a brilliant man, undoubtedly the most inspired intellect of the thirteenth century. Yet history does not know him. Only I do, and my memories of him are filled with sorrow.

I met him after Mass one day. I despised the Church, but enjoyed the actual service. All the chanting, the choirs, and I loved to hear the early organs played. Often I would go to communion, after attending confession. It was difficult for me to keep a straight face while I told of my sins. Once, for fun, I told a priest the *whole* truth of what I had done in my life. But he was drunk and just said to do five Hail Marys and to behave myself. I didn't have to kill him.

I received the Holy Eucharist from Arturo and met him after the service. I could tell he was attracted to me. In those days many priests had mistresses. I had gone out of my way to see Arturo because a gypsy healer had told me about him. He was an alchemist, she said, who could turn stone into gold, sunlight into ideas, moonlight into lust. The gypsy had a high opinion of Arturo. She warned me to approach him cautiously because his real work had to be kept from the Church. I understood.

Commonly, an alchemist is known as an esoteric chemist who attempts to convert base metals into gold. This is a crude understanding. Alchemy is a comprehensive physical and metaphysical system embracing cosmology as much as anthropology. Everything natural and supernatural can be found in it. The goal of alchemy is to experience the totality of the organism. It is a path of enlightenment. The gypsy said Arturo was a born alchemist. Knowledge came to him from inside. No one had to teach him his art.

"The only trouble with him is he's a Catholic," she said. "A fanatic."

"How does he merge the two disciplines?" I asked.

The gypsy blessed herself. She was superstitious of the Church as well. "God only knows," she said.

Arturo did not strike me as a fanatic when we first met. His demeanor was soft, like his lovely eyes. He had a special ability to listen totally to a person, a rare gift. His large hands were exceptionally fine; when he brushed my arm with his fingers I felt he was capable of touching my heart. And he was so young! That first afternoon we talked about astronomy—a midway subject, in my mind, to alchemy. He was delighted with my knowledge of the heavens. He invited me to share a meal and afterward we went for a walk around the city. When we said goodbye that night, I knew he was in love with me.

Why did I pursue him? For the same reason I have done many things in my life—I was curious. But that was only my initial reason. Soon I, too, was in love with him. I must say, the feeling was present before I began to probe his knowledge of alchemy. Before going that deep into his secret world, I knew he was unlike other priests of his day. He was a virgin, and his vow of celibacy was important to him.

I did not just spring the questions on him one day. Can you turn copper into gold? Can you heal lepers? Can you live forever? I showed him a glimpse of my knowledge first, to inspire him to share his. My understanding of the medical properties of herbs is extensive. An old friar in Arturo's church became ill with a lung infection, and it seemed as if he'd die. I brought Arturo an herb concoction of echinacea and goldenseal and told him to give it to his superior. The friar recovered within twenty-four hours and

Arturo wanted to know who had taught me how to make tea.

I laughed and told him about my Greek friend, Cleo, failing to mention how many centuries ago he had died. Arturo was impressed. It was only then he began to talk about his crystals and magnets and copper sheets—the secret elements of alchemy that have now passed from human understanding. That very day Arturo confessed his mission in life to me. To discover the elixirs of holiness and immortality—as if searching for the secret to one of these conditions was not enough. Arturo always thought big. He was determined to re-create nothing less than the blood of Jesus Christ.

"What makes you think you can do it?" I asked, shocked.

His eyes shone as he explained. Not with a mad light, but with a brilliance I had never seen before or since in a mortal man.

"Because I have found the spirit of man," he said. "I have proven that it exists. I can show you how to experience it, how to remove the veil of darkness that covers it."

Sounded interesting to me. Arturo took me to a secret chamber beneath the church where he lived. Apparently the elderly friar whose life I had saved knew of Arturo's hobby and looked the other way. He was the only one who knew of the master alchemist, besides the gypsy. I asked Arturo about her. Apparently she had nursed him back to health when he had fallen from a horse while riding in the countryside.

They had shared many intimate conversations over late-night fires. Arturo was surprised, and a bit angry, that she had told me about him.

"Don't blame her," I said. "I can be most persuasive." It was true that I had used the power of my eyes on her, when I saw she was hiding something important.

Arturo took me down into his secret room and lit many candles. He asked me to lie on a huge copper sheet, as thin as modern paper. On adjacent shelves, I noted his collection of quartz crystals, amethysts, and precious stones—rubies, diamonds, and sapphires. He also had several powerful magnets, each cut into the shape of a cross. I had never seen a magnetic cross before.

"What are you going to do?" I asked as I lay down on the copper.

"You have heard of the human aura?" he asked.

"Yes. It is the energy field that surrounds the body."

"Very good. It is spoken of in ancient mythology and is present in art. We see the halos in paintings above the heads of members of the holy family, and in drawings of saints. Still, most people don't believe in the aura because they don't experience it. They are only conscious of their physical bodies. What I am going to do to you now is draw out your aura, allow your consciousness to expand into it, so that your spiritual body becomes the focus of your attention, and not the physical body."

"Do you not like my physical body?" I asked. I often flirted with him.

He paused and stared down at me. "It's very lovely," he whispered.

He told me to close my eyes. He didn't want me to see how he set up the crystals and magnets. I peeked, of course, and saw that crystals were placed above my head and magnets below my body, at angles. He was creating a grid of some kind, one that transmitted unseen energies. He prayed as he worked, Hail Marys and Our Fathers. I have always enjoyed those prayers. But for me, of course, they reminded me of Radha and Krishna.

When Arturo was done, he told me to keep my eyes closed and breathe naturally through my nose. The breath was important, he said. It was one of the secrets of experiencing the soul.

For the first few minutes not much happened. But then, slowly, I felt an energy rise from my body, from the base of my spine to the top of my head. Simultaneously, I felt my mind expand. I became as big as the secret chamber. A curious floating sensation enveloped me, a warm peacefulness. My breath went in and out, sometimes fast, sometimes slow. I had no control over it and wanted none. Time passed. I wasn't entirely awake, but I wasn't asleep either. It was a mystical experience.

When Arturo spoke next, he sounded many miles away. He wanted me to sit up, to come out of the state. I resisted—I liked where I was. But he took my arm and forced me to sit up, breaking the spell. I opened my eyes and gazed at him.

"Why did you stop it?" I asked.

He was perspiring. "You can get too much energy at once." He stared at me; he seemed out of breath. "You have an amazing aura."

I smiled. "What is special about it?"

He shook his head. "It is so powerful."

The experiment in consciousness raising was interesting, but I failed to see how his technique would allow him to transform human blood into Christ's blood. I quizzed him about it at length but he would divulge no more secrets. The power of my aura continued to puzzle him. As we said good night, I saw fear in his eyes, and deep fascination. He knew I was no ordinary woman. That was all right, I thought. No harm done. He would learn no more about my special qualities.

But that was not to be.

He was to learn everything about me.

Perhaps even more than I knew myself.

There was an altar boy, Ralphe, who lived with the priests. Twelve years old and possessed of an exceptional wit, he was a favorite of Arturo's. Often the two would go for long hikes in the hills outside Florence. I was fond of Ralphe myself. The three of us had picnics in the woods and I would teach Ralphe the flute, for which he had a talent. The instrument had been a favorite of mine since the day I met Krishna. Arturo used to love to watch us play together. But sometimes I would get carried away and weave a melody of love, of romantic enchantment and lost dreams, which would always leave Arturo quiet and shaken. How long we could go on like this, chaste and virtuous, I didn't know. My alchemist stirred ancient longings inside me. I wondered about the energies his crystals invoked.

One day while I was helping Ralphe repair a hole in the church roof, the boy decided to amuse me by doing a silly dance on the edge of the stone tiles. I told him to be careful but he never listened. He was having too much fun. That is the mysterious thing about tragedy—it often strikes at the happiest moment.

Ralphe slipped and fell. It was over a hundred feet to the ground. He fell on the base of his spine, crushing it. When I reached him, he was writhing in agony. I was shaken to the core, I who had seen so much pain in my life. But centuries of time have not made me insensitive. One moment he had been a vibrant young man, and now he would be crippled for the rest of his days, and those would not be long.

I loved Ralphe very much. He was like a son to me.

I suppose that's why I did what I did.

I did not need to make him a vampire to help him.

I opened the veins on my right wrist and let the blood splash where his shattered spinal column had pierced his skin. The wound closed quickly, the bones mended. It seemed he would make a complete recovery. Best of all, he appeared unaware of why he had recovered so quickly. He thought he'd just been lucky.

But there is good luck and bad luck.

Arturo saw what I did for Ralphe. He saw everything.

He wanted to know who I was. What I was.

I find it hard to lie to those I love.

I told him everything. Even what Krishna had told me. The tale took an entire night. Arturo understood when I was through why I preferred to tell the story in the dark. But he didn't recoil in horror as I spoke. He was an enlightened priest, an alchemist who sought the answer to why God had created us in the first place. Indeed, he thought he knew the answer to that profound question. We were here to become like God. To live like his blessed son. We just needed a few pints of Christ's blood to do it.

Arturo believed Krishna had let me live for a purpose.

So that my blood could save mankind from itself.

From the start, I worried about him mixing Christ and vampires.

"But I will make no more vampires," I protested.

He eagerly took my hands and stared into my eyes. A fever burned in his brain; I could feel the heat of it on his fingertips, in his breath. Whose soul did I experience then? Mine or his? It seemed in that moment as if the two of us had merged. For that reason, his next words sounded inevitable to me.

"We will make no more vampires," he said. "I understand why Krishna made you take such a vow. What we will create with your blood is a new man. A hybrid of a human and a vampire. A being who can live forever, in the glory of light instead of the shadow of darkness." His eyes strayed to the wooden crucifix hung above his bed. "An immortal being."

He spoke with such power. And he was not insane. I had to listen. To consider his words.

"Is it possible?" I whispered.

"Yes." He hugged me. "There is a secret I haven't told you. It is extraordinary. It is the secret to permanent transformation. If I have the right materials—your blood, for example—I can transform anything. If you wish, you can become such a hybrid. I can even make you human again." He paused, perhaps thinking of my ancient grief over the loss of Lalita, my daughter. He knew my sterile condition was the curse of my unending life. He must have known, since he added, "You could have a child, Sita."

5

Around midnight I return to the compound, determined to learn its layout from the outside. Dressed totally in black, I have an Uzi strung over my back, a high-powered pair of binoculars in one hand, a Geiger counter in the other. The momentary phenomenon of my glowing skin continues to haunt me. I wonder if they are doing something weird to Joel—using radiation on him.

I have decided the ideal vantage point from which to study the compound is the top of the hill in which the base is dug. To get to it I have to take a long walk. Here the terrain is even too rough for my new Jeep. I move swiftly, my head down, like the mystical serpent I embody. A deep desire to plant my teeth in that general I saw the past night stays with me. He reminds me of Eddie—not of the psycho's warped nature but of his delusions of grandeur. I can tell a lot by a man's face. Perhaps I read his mind a little as well. The general wants to use Joel to get ahead in the world, maybe take it over. I don't know where the Pentagon gets these people.

At the top of the hill I scan each square foot of the compound. Once again I am stunned by the level of security. It is as if they are set up to ward off an attack from an alien race. While I watch, a sleek jet with the lines of a rocket lands on the runway. It is like no jet I have ever seen before, and I suspect it can do Mach 10—ten times the speed of sound—and that Congress has never heard of it.

My Geiger counter indicates the radiation here is three times what is normal, but still well within safety limits. I'm puzzled. Radiation couldn't have been responsible for my luminous skin. Yet the fact that the level is high confirms that there are nuclear warheads in the vicinity. I suspect I am sitting above them, that they are stored in the caves the military has dug into this hill. The caves are now an established fact. I watch as men and equipment ride a miniature railroad beneath me into and out of the hill. This is how the human race gets into trouble. The danger of renegade vampires is nothing compared to the folly of handing unlimited sums of money over to people who like to keep "secrets." Who have on their payroll physicists and chemists and genetic engineers who, as children, rooted for Pandora to open her box of evils.

How Andrew Kane has partially managed to duplicate Arturo Evola's work continues to preoccupy me. I cannot imagine an explanation.

A black cart rides beneath me into the hill. Soldiers sit on it, smoking cigarettes and talking about babes. My Geiger counter momentarily jumps. The level is not high enough to harm the human body, but it does confirm that the boys in uniform are sitting next to a thermonuclear device. I know the famed fail-safe system is a joke, as do most people in the government. The President of the United States is not the only one who can order an American-made nuclear device to explode. In West Germany, before the Wall came down, the authority to fire a miniature neutron bomb was often in the hands of a lieutenant. Currently, *all* the nuclear submarine captains in the U.S. Navy have the authority to launch their missiles without the required presidential black box and secret codes. It is argued that the captains must have this authority because if the country is attacked the President would most likely be one of the first to die.

Still, it makes me nervous.

The general must have the authority to trigger these bombs if he wishes.

It is good to know.

I have finished my study of the compound and am walking back to my Jeep when I notice that my legs are glowing again, as are my hands and arms. Once more, every square inch of my exposed skin is faintly shining with the whiteness of the moon—not good here at a top-secret camp. It makes me that much more visible. I hurry to my Jeep, climb inside, and drive away.

But long before I reach Las Vegas, I pull over, far off the road.

A bizarre idea has occurred to me.

The problem is not radiation. It is not man-made.

Climbing out of the Jeep, I remove all my clothing and stand naked with my arms outstretched to the moon, as if I were worshipping the astronomical satellite, bowing to it, drinking up her rays. Slowly the skin on my chest and thighs begins to take on the milky radiance. And it seems the more I invite the moonlight onto my skin, *into* my heart, the brighter it becomes. Because if I will it to stop, my skin returns to normal.

"What does it mean, Yaksha?" I whisper to my dead creator.

My right arm, as the moonlight floods in, shines particularly bright. Holding it close to my eyes, *I can see through it!* I can actually see the ground through my flesh!

I put my clothes back on.

I can't look like a Christmas light when I try to seduce Andrew Kane.

6

I am Lara Adams as I enter the casino later that night
and stand beside Andrew Kane at the dice table. I'm
still a redhead, with a soft southern accent and a prim
and proper smile. The name is not new to me. I used it
to enroll at Mayfair High in Oregon, where I met Ray
and Seymour. It's hard to believe that was less than
two months ago. How life can change when you're a
vampire on the run.

Andy glances over at me and smiles. He has the dice
in his hands. He has been in the casino five minutes
but already he's had a couple of drinks.

"Do you want to place a bet?" he asks.

I smile. "Do you feel hot?"

He shakes the dice in his palm. "I *am* hot."

I remove a stack of black hundred-dollar chips from

71

my bag and place one on the pass line, his favorite bet—seven or eleven. Andy rolls the dice. They dance over the green felt. Coming to a halt, the numbers four and three smile up at us.

"Lucky seven," the croupier says and pays off our bets. Andy flashes me another smile.

"You must be good luck," he says.

I double my bet. "I have a feeling this is my night," I say.

By the time the dice come to me, Andy and I have lost a combined total of eight hundred dollars. That is about to change. With my supernatural balance and reflexes, with practice, I can roll any number I desire. I have been practicing in my suite since I returned from the compound. Carefully I set the dice upright in my left palm in the configuration: five and six. In a blur, I toss them out. They bounce happily, seemingly randomly to human eyes. But they come to a halt in the same position they started out. Andy and I each win a hundred dollars on the number eleven. Since I threw a pass, I am invited to throw another—which I do. The people at the table like me. Most bet on the pass line.

I throw ten passes in a row before I let the dice go. We mustn't get greedy. Andy appreciates my style.

"What's your name?" he asks.

"Lara Adams. What's yours?"

"Andrew Kane. Are you here alone?"

I pout. "I did come with a friend. But it seems I'll be going home alone."

Andy chuckles. "Not necessarily. The night's still young."

"It's five in the morning," I remind him.

He nods at the glass of water I sip. "Can I get you something stronger?"

I lean against the table. "I think I need something stronger."

We continue to play craps, winning better than honest wages when I am throwing the dice. The people at the table don't want me to surrender the designated high roller position, but I am careful not to appear superhuman, just damn lucky. Andy bets heavily and wins back all the money he lost the night before, and then some. We both drink too much. I have four margaritas, Andy five Scotches and water, on top of what he had drunk before I entered. The alcohol has no effect on me. My liver neutralizes it almost the instant it enters my system. I can take in all kinds of poisons and remain undisturbed. Andy, however, is now drunk, just the way the casinos like people. He is betting five hundred dollars a roll when I pull him away from the table.

"What's the matter?" he protests. "We're winning."

"You can be winning and courting disaster at the same time. Come on, let's have some coffee. I'm buying."

He stumbles as he walks beside me. "I've been at work all night. I'd like a steak."

"You shall have whatever you want."

The Mirage coffee shop is open twenty-four hours a

day. The menu is flexible—Andy is able to get his steak. He orders it medium rare with a baked potato. He wants a beer, but I insist he have a glass of milk.

"You're going to destroy your stomach," I say as we wait for our food. I do have favorite foods, besides blood. I have ordered roast chicken with rice and vegetable. Surprisingly, for a vampire, I eat plenty of vegetables. Nothing is as good for the body as those fresh greens, except, perhaps, those dripping reds. Sitting with Andy, I become thirsty for blood as well. Before I rest, I will grab some male tourist off the streets, show him a good time. That is, if I don't spend the night—the day—sleeping beside Andy. His eyes shine as he looks me over.

"I can always have it removed," he replies.

"Why not just drink less?"

"I'm on vacation."

"Where are you from?"

He chuckles. "Here!" He is serious for a moment. "You know you are one beautiful young woman. But I suppose you know that."

"It's always nice to hear."

"Where are you from?"

"The South—Florida. I came with a boyfriend for a few days, but he got angry with me."

"Why?"

"I told him I wanted to break up." I add, "He's got a nasty temper." I sip my milk, wishing I could squeeze our waitress's veins into it, add a little flavor. "What about you? What do you do?"

"I'm a mad scientist."

74

"Really? What are you mad about?"

"You mean, what kind of scientist am I?"

"Yes. And do you work around here?"

His voice takes on a guarded note, even though he is still quite drunk. "I'm a genetic engineer. I work for the government. They have a lab—in town."

I mock him playfully. "Is it a top-secret lab?"

He sits back and shrugs. "They would like to keep it that way. They don't feel comfortable unless we're working outside the reach of mainstream scientists."

"Do I detect a note of resentment in your tone?"

"Not resentment—that's too strong a word. I love my job. It has provided me opportunities I couldn't get in the normal business world. I think what you sense is frustration. The opportunities presented in our lab are not being fully exploited. We need people of many disciplines involved, from all over the world."

"You would like the lab to be more open?"

"Precisely. But that doesn't mean I don't appreciate the need for security." He pauses. "Especially as of late."

"Interesting things are happening?"

He looks away and chuckles, but there is a note of sorrow in his voice. "Very interesting things." He turns back to me. "May I ask you a personal question, Lara?"

"By all means."

"How old are you?"

I flirt. "How old do you think I am?"

He is genuinely puzzled. "I don't know. When we

were at the table, you seemed about thirty. But now that we're alone together you seem much younger."

I have designed my makeup and dress to appear older. My longish white dress is conservative; I have a strand of pearls around my neck. My lipstick is glossy, overdone. I wear a red scarf to match my red wig.

"I'm twenty-nine," I say, which is the age on my new driver's license and passport. "I appreciate your compliment, however. I take care of myself." I pause. "How old are you?"

He laughs, picking up his glass of milk. "Let's just say my liver would be a lot younger if this was all I drank."

"'Milk does a body good.'"

He sets the glass down and stares into it. "So do other things."

"Andy?"

He shakes his head. "Just something that's going on at work. I can't talk about it. It would bore you anyway." He changes the subject. "Where did you learn to throw dice like that?"

"Like what?"

"Come on. You always throw them the same way, resting the number you want to come up on your open palm. How do you do it? I've never seen anyone who could control the bounce of the dice."

I realize I went too far. He is a smart man, I remind myself. His powers of observation are keen, even when he is intoxicated. Yet, at the same time I don't mind that he sees something special in me. I have no time to cultivate his interest slowly. I must have him under my thumb by tomorrow night. It is then I plan to rescue Joel.

I answer his question carefully. "I have had many interesting teachers. Perhaps I could tell you about them sometime."

"How about now, tonight?"

"Tonight? The sun will be up in an hour."

"I don't have to be at work until it goes down." He reaches across the table and takes my hand. "I like you, Lara. I mean that." He pauses. "I feel like I've met you before."

I shake my head, wondering if he senses the similarities between Joel and myself. "We have never met," I tell him.

7

We go back to his place. He offers me a drink. When I decline, he has one himself—a Scotch on the rocks. The food in his stomach has sobered him up somewhat, but he quickly proceeds to get drunk again. He has a real problem, and now it is my problem as well. Granted, his intoxicated state makes his tongue loose and he tells me far more about his work than he should, although he has yet to mention Joel or vampires. Still, I will need him clear headed to help me. I have no time to repair his wounded psyche. I wonder what makes him drink so much. He lied when he said he didn't resent his boss. Obviously he hates the general. But I cannot read his mind, probably because he keeps it scrambled with booze. I sense only deep emotional conflicts, coupled with intellectual excitement. He is grateful to be working on Joel, analyzing his blood, and yet it bothers him that he is directly involved in the project. I have no doubt of this.

We sit on the couch in the living room. He riffles through his mail and then throws it on the floor. "Bills," he mutters, sipping his drink. "The hardest reality of life, besides death."

"The way you gamble, I hope the government pays you well."

He snorts softly, staring at the eastern sky, which has begun to brighten. "They don't pay me what I'm worth, that's for sure." He glances at my strand of pearls. "You look like you don't have to worry about money."

"Daddy made millions in oil before he died." I shrug. "I was his only child."

"He left it all to you?"

"Every last penny."

"Must be nice."

"It is very nice." I move closer to him on the sofa, touch his knee. I have an alluring touch. I swear sometimes I could seduce an evangelist's wife as easily as I could a horny Marine. Sex holds no mystery for me, and I have no scruples. I use my body as easily as any other weapon. I add, "What exactly do you do at your lab?"

He gestures to his office. "It's in there."

"What's in there?"

He takes another swallow of Scotch. "My greatest

discovery. I keep a model of it at home to inspire me."
He burps. "But right now a fat raise would inspire me
more."

Even though I know what's in his office, I walk over
and have a peep at the two models of the DNA, the
human one and the vampiric molecule. "What are
they?" I ask.

He is enjoying his drink too much to get up. "Have
you heard of DNA?"

"Yes, of course. I graduated from college."

"What school did you go to?"

"Florida State." I return to my place on the couch,
closer to him than before. "I graduated with honors."

"What was your major?"

"English lit, but I took several biology classes. I
know that DNA is a double helix molecule that
encodes all the information necessary for life to
exist." I pause. "Are those models of human DNA?"

He sets his drink down. "One of them is."

"What's the other one?"

He stretches and yawns. "A project my partners and
I have been working on for the last month."

My blood turns cold. It was in the last month
that Eddie began to produce his horde of vampiric gangbangers. Andy has been able to duplicate
Arturo's visions of vampire DNA because he has been
analyzing the molecules for a while, long before Joel
was captured. That can only mean one of Eddie's
offspring escaped my slaughter.

"I don't know. I destroyed your silly gang."

"You're not sure of that."

"Now I am sure. You see, I can tell when someone lies. It's one of those great gifts I possess that you don't. There is only you left, and we both know it."

"What of it? I can make more whenever I feel the need."

Eddie admitted that there were no others. He couldn't have tricked me, yet perhaps he himself was tricked. Maybe one of *his* offspring had made another vampire and didn't tell him. It's the only explanation. That vampire must have been caught by the government and taken to the desert compound. I wonder if the mystery vampire is still in the place. My rescue effort has just been complicated.

I have to wonder if I'm already too late. Andy has—at the least—an outline of the DNA code of the vampire. How long will it be before he and his partners are able to create more bloodsuckers? The only thing that gives me hope is that the general struck me as a man who keeps everything under wraps, until it is time to make his move. Andy has said as much about him. Everything connected to vampires is still probably locked up in the compound.

In response to Andy's comment, I force a chuckle. Boy, do I force it. "Are you making a modern Frankenstein monster?" I ask, kidding, but not kidding.

My question hits a nerve, for obvious reasons, and Andy sits quietly for a moment, staring at his drink as if it were a crystal ball.

"We are playing a high-stakes game," he admits.

"Altering the DNA code of any species is like rolling the dice. You can win and you can lose."

"But it must be exciting to be playing such a game?"

He sighs. "We have the wrong pit boss in charge."

I put my hand on his shoulder. "What's his name?"

"General Havor. He's a hard ass—I don't think his mother gave him a first name. At least I don't know it. We call him 'General' or 'Sir.' He believes in order, performance, sacrifice, discipline, power." Andy shakes his head. "He definitely doesn't create an environment for free thinking and loving cooperation."

I am the understanding girlfriend. "You should quit then."

Andy flashes an amused, bitter grin. "If I quit now I'd be walking away from one of the greatest discoveries of modern time. Plus I need the job. I need the money."

I caress his hair. My voice is soft and seductive. "You need to relax, Andy, and not think of this stupid general. Tell you what—when you get off work tomorrow, come straight to my suite. I'm staying at the Mirage, Room Two-One-Three-Four. We can play the tables and have another late dinner together."

Gently he takes my hand. His eyes momentarily come into focus, and I see his intellect again, feel his warmth. He is a good man, working in a bad place.

"Do you have to go now?" he asks sadly.

I lean over and kiss him on the cheek. "Yes. But

we'll see each other tomorrow." I sit back and wink. "We'll have fun."

He is pleased. "You know what I like about you, Lara?"

"What?"

"You have a good heart. I feel I can trust you."

I nod. "You can trust me, Andy. You really can."

8 ∼∼∼

One of the saddest stories told in modern literature, to me at least, is Mary Shelley's *Frankenstein*. Because in a sense I am that monster. Knowingly or unknowingly, to much of history, I am the inspiration of nightmares. I am the primeval fear, something dead come to life, or better yet—and more accurate—something that refuses to die. Yet I consider myself more human than Shelley's creation, more humane than Arturo's offspring. I am a monster, but I can also love deeply. Yet even my love for Arturo could not spare him from plunging us into a nightmare from which there seemed to be no waking.

His secret of transformation was very simple, and profound beyond belief. It is fashionable among New Age adherents to use crystals to develop higher states of consciousness. What most of these people do not know is that a crystal is merely an amplifier, and that it has to be used very carefully. Whatever is present in the aura of the person, in the psychic field, gets magnified. Hate can be boosted as easily as compassion. In fact, cruel emotions expand more easily when given the chance. Arturo had an intuitive sense of the proper crystal to use with each person. Indeed, on most people he refused to use crystals at all. Few, he said, were ready for such high vibrations. How tragic it was that when he had a vial of my blood in his hand, his intuition deserted him. It is a pity his special genius did not leave him as well. It took a genius to take us as far as he did.

A mad one.

Using the magnets and copper sheets, in his secret geometric arrangements, the vibrations from whatever Arturo placed over the person were transmitted into the aura. For example, when he placed a clear quartz crystal above my head, a deep peaceful state settled in my mind. Yet if he used a similar crystal with young Ralphe, the boy would become irritated. Ralphe had too much going on in his mind and was not ready for crystals. Arturo understood that. He was an alchemist in the truest sense of the word. He could transform what could not be changed. Souls as well as bodies.

Arturo did not believe the body created the mind. He felt it was the other way around, and I believe he was correct. When he altered an aura, he changed the person's physiology as well. He just needed the proper materials, he said, to change anything. A flawed human into a glorious god. A sterile vampire into a loving mother.

It was, in the end, the chance to become human again that caused me to give him my blood. To hold *my* daughter in *my* hands again—what ecstasy! I was seduced by ancient griefs. Yaksha had made me pay dearly for my immortality, with the loss of Rama and Lalita. Arturo promised to give me back half of what had been stolen. It had been over four thousand years. Half seemed better than nothing. As I let my blood drip into a gold communion chalice for Arturo, I prayed to Krishna to bless it.

"I am not breaking my vow to you," I whispered, not believing my own words. "I am just trying to break this curse."

I did not know, as I prayed to my God, that Arturo was also praying to his. To allow him to convert human and vampiric blood into the saving fluid of Jesus Christ. Genius may make a person a fanatic, I don't know. But I do know that a fanatic will never listen to anything other than his own dreams. Arturo was soft and kind, warm and loving. Yet he was convinced he had a great destiny. Hitler thought the same. Both wanted something nature had never granted—the perfect being. And I, the ancient monster, just wanted a child. Arturo and I—we should never have met.

But perhaps our meeting was destined.

My blood looked so dark in the chalice.

The sacredness of the chalice did nothing to dispel my gloom.

Arturo wanted to place my blood above the head of select humans. To merge the vibration of my immortal pattern into that of a mortal. If he changed the aura, he said, the body would be transformed. He, of all people, should have known how potent my blood was. He had stared deep into my eyes. He should have known my will would not bend easily to the will of another.

"You will not put the blood in their veins?" I asked as I handed him the chalice. He shook his head.

"Never," he promised. "Your God and my God are the same. Your vow will remain unbroken."

"I'm not fooling myself," I said quietly. "I have broken a portion of it." I moved close to him. "I do this for you."

He touched me then—he rarely did, before that night. It was hard for him to feel my flesh and not burn. "You do this for yourself as well," he said.

I loved to stare deeply into his eyes. "That is true. But as I do this—for you as well as for myself—you must do likewise."

He wanted to draw back but he only came closer. "What do you mean?"

I kissed him then, for the first time, on the cheek. "You have to break your vow. You have to make love to me."

His eyes were round. "I can't. My life is dedicated to Christ."

I did not smile. His words were not funny, but tragic. The seed of all that was to follow was hidden inside them. But I did not see that then, at least not clearly. I just wanted him so badly. I kissed him again, on the lips.

"You believe my blood will lead you to Christ," I said. "I do not know about that. But I do know where I can take you." I set down the bloody chalice and my arms went around him, the wings of the vampire swallowing its prey. "Pretend I am your God, Arturo, at least for tonight. I will make it easy for you."

There was one last ingredient in Arturo's technique that I did not witness during my first session. While I was lying on the floor with all the paraphernalia around me, he had set a mirror above the crystals. This mirror was coordinated with an external mirror, which allowed moonlight to shine through the crystals. It was actually the light, altered by its passage through the quartz medium, that set in motion the higher vibration in the aura that altered the body. Arturo never focused the sun directly through the crystals, saying it would be much too powerful. Of course, Arturo understood that the light of the moon was identical to the light of the sun, only softened by cosmic reflection.

Arturo made with his own hands a crystal vial to hold my blood.

His first experiment was with a local child who had been retarded since birth. The boy lived on the streets and existed on the scraps of food tossed to him by strangers. It was my desire that Arturo first work on someone who couldn't turn him over to the Inquisition. Still, Arturo was taking a big risk experimenting on anyone. The Church would have burned him at the stake. How I hated its self-righteous dogma, its hypocrisy. Arturo never knew how many inquisitors I killed—a small detail that I forgot to mention in my confession to him.

I remember well how gently Arturo spoke to the child to get him to relax on the copper sheet. Normally the boy was filthy, but I had given him a bath before the beginning of the experiment. He was naturally distrustful of others, having been abused so many times during his life. But he liked us—I had been feeding him off and on and Arturo had a way with children. Soon enough, he was lying on the copper and breathing comfortably. The reflected moonlight, peering through the dark vial of my blood, cast a haunting red hue over the room. It reminded me of the end of twilight, of the time just before night falls.

"Something is happening," Arturo whispered as we watched the boy's breathing accelerate. For twenty minutes the child was in a state of hyperventilation, twitching and shaking. We would have stopped the process if the boy's face hadn't looked calm. Plus, we were watching history being made, maybe a miracle.

Finally the boy lay still. Arturo diverted the reflected moonlight and helped the boy to sit up. There was a new strangeness to his eyes—they were bright. He hugged me.

"Ti amo anch'io, Sita," he said. *"I love you, Sita."* I

had never heard him say a whole sentence before. I was so overjoyed that I didn't stop to think I had never told him my real name. In all of Italy, only Arturo and Ralphe knew it. We were both happy for the child, that his brain seemed to be functioning normally. It was one of the few times in my life I cried, tears of water, not tears of blood.

The red tears would come later.

This first successful experiment gave Arturo tremendous confidence and weakened his caution. He had seen a mental change; he wanted to see a physical one. He went looking for a leper, and brought back a woman in her sixties whose toes and fingers had been eaten away by the dread disease. Over the centuries I had found it particularly painful to look upon lepers. In the second century, in Rome, I had a beautiful lover who developed leprosy. Toward the latter stages of his disease, he begged me to kill him, and I did, crushing his skull, with my eyes tightly clenched. Of course, now there is AIDS. Mother Nature gives each age its own special horror. She is like Lord Krishna, full of wicked surprises.

The woman was almost too far gone to notice what we were doing to her. But Arturo was able to get her breathing deeply, and soon the magic was happening again. She began to hyperventilate, twitching worse than the boy had. Yet her eyes and face remained calm. I was not sure what she felt; it was not as if she suddenly sprouted toes and fingers. When she was through, Arturo led her upstairs and had her lie down on a bed. But from the start she did seem stronger, more alert.

A few days later she began to grow toes and fingers. Two weeks later there was no sign of her leprosy.

Arturo was ecstatic, but I was worried. We told the woman not to tell anyone what we had done for her. Of course she told *everyone*. The rumors started to fly. Wisely, Arturo passed her cure off to the grace of God. Yet, during these days of the Inquisition, it was more dangerous to be a saint than a sinner. A sinner, as long as he or she was not a heretic, could repent and escape with a flogging. A saint might be a witch. Better to burn a possible saint, the Church thought, than let a genuine witch escape. They had a weird sense of justice.

Arturo was not a complete fool, however. He did not heal more lepers, even though dozens came to his door seeking relief. Yet he continued to experiment on a few deaf and dumb people, a few who were actually retarded. Oh, but it was hard to turn away the lepers. The lone woman had given them such hope. Modern-day pundits often talk of the virtue of hope. To me, hope brings grief. The most content people are those who expect nothing, who have ceased to dream.

I had dreamed what it would be like to be Arturo's lover, and now that he was mine, he was unhappy. Oh, he loved to sleep with me, feel me close beside him. But he believed he had sinned and he couldn't stop. The timing of our affair was unfortunate. He was breaking his vow of celibacy just when he was on the verge of fulfilling his destiny. God would not know whether to curse or bless him. I told him not to worry about God. I had met the guy. He did what he wanted when he wanted, no matter how hard you tried. I told Arturo many stories of Krishna, and he listened, fascinated. Still, he would weep after we had sex. I told him to go to confession. But he refused—he would only confess to me. Only I could understand him, he said.

But I didn't understand. Not what he had planned.

He began to have visions during this period. He'd had them before—they didn't alarm me, at least not at first. It was a vision that had given him the mechanics of his transformative technique, long before we met. But now his visions were peculiar. He began to build models. Only seven hundred years later did I realize he was building models of DNA—human DNA, vampiric, and one other form. Yes, it is true, while we watched the people twitch on the floor under the influence of my bloody aura, Arturo saw more deeply than I did. He actually understood the specific molecule whose code defined the body. He saw the molecule in a vision, and he watched it change under the magnets, crystals, copper, and blood. He saw the double helix of normal DNA. He saw the twelve straight strands of my DNA. And he saw how the two could be conjoined.

"We need twelve helix strands," he confided in me. "Then we will have our perfect being."

"But the more people you experiment on, the more

attention you will draw to yourself," I protested. "Your Church will not understand. They will kill you."

He nodded grimly. "I understand. And I cannot keep working on abnormal people. To make a leap toward the perfect being, I must work with a normal person."

I sensed what was in his mind. "You cannot experiment on yourself."

He turned away. "What if we try Ralphe?"

"No," I pleaded. "We love him the way he is. Let's not change him."

He continued to stare at the wall, his back to me. "You changed him, Sita."

"That was different. I knew what I was doing. I had experience. I healed his wounds. I altered his body, not his soul."

He turned to me. "Don't you see it's because I love Ralphe as much as you do that I want to give him this chance? If we can change him from the inside out, transform his blood, he will be like a child of Christ."

"Christ never knew of vampires," I warned. "You should not mix the two in your mind. It's blasphemy —even to me."

Arturo was passionate. "How do you know he didn't? You never met him."

I got angry. "Now you speak like a fool. If you want to experiment on anyone, use me. You promised me you would when we started this."

He stiffened. "I can't change you. Not now."

I understood what he was saying. Suddenly I felt the weight of shattered dreams. In my mind I had been playing with a daughter who had never been born, and who probably never would be.

"You need my blood first," I replied. "The pure vampire blood." It was true he had to replenish the blood in the crystal vial, not before each experiment, but often. Old blood did not work—it was too dead. I continued, "But what if your experiment does work and you do create a perfect being? I cannot give enough blood to alter everyone on this planet."

He shrugged. "Perhaps those who are altered can become the new donors."

"That is a huge *perhaps*. Also, I know people. This will be an exclusive club. It doesn't matter how good your intentions are now." I turned away and chuckled bitterly. "Who will be given a chance at perfection? The nobility? The clergy? The most corrupt will feel they are the most deserving. It is the oldest lesson of history. It never changes."

Arturo hugged me. "That will not happen, Sita. God has blessed this work. Only good can come from it."

"No one knows what God has blessed," I whispered. "And what he has cursed."

A few days went by during which Arturo and I hardly spoke. He would stay up late making models of molecules no one had seen, afraid to talk to me, to touch me. I never realized until then how he saw me as both a gift and a test from God. Of course I had given him my immortal perception on the matter, but he had seen me that way from the start. I brought him magic blood *and* delicious sensuality. He was supposed to take one and not the other, he thought. He lost his intuitive sense that kept him from mistakes, I believe, because he no longer thought he was worthy of having it. He stopped praying to God and started muttering to himself about the blood of Jesus Christ. He was more obsessed with blood than I was, and I had it for dinner every few days.

One evening I could find Ralphe nowhere. Arturo said he had no idea where he was. Arturo wasn't lying, but he wasn't telling the whole truth either. I didn't press him. I think I didn't want to know the truth. Yet had I insisted he tell me, I might have stopped the horror, before it got out of hand.

The screams started in the middle of night.

I was out for a walk at the time. It was my custom to go out late, disguised, find a homeless person, drink a pint of blood, whisper in his or her ear, and put the person back to sleep. Except for evil priests, I didn't often kill in those days. The cries that came to me that night chilled me through. I ran toward the sounds as fast as I could.

I found five bodies, horribly mangled, their limbs torn off. Obviously, only a being of supernatural strength could have committed these acts. One person, a woman with an arm lying beside her, was the last one still alive. I cradled her head in my lap.

"What happened?" I asked. "Who did this to you?"

"The demon," she whispered.

"What did this demon look like?" I demanded.

She gagged. "A hungry angel. The blood—" Her eyes strayed to her severed arm and she wept. "My blood."

I shook her. "Tell me what this demon looked like?"

Her eyes rolled up into her head. "A child," she whispered with her last breath and died in my arms.

Sick at heart, I knew who the child was.

Far away, on the far side of the town, I heard more screams.

I flew toward them but once again I was too late. There were more shredded bodies, and this time there were witnesses. An angry mob with burning torches was gathering. They had seen the demon child.

"It was heading for the woods!" they cried.

"We have to stop it!" others cried.

"Wait!" I yelled. "Look how many it has killed. We can't go after it without help."

"It killed my brother!" one man cried, pulling out a knife. "I'm going to kill it myself."

The mob followed the man. I had no choice but to tag along. As we wound through the dark streets, we found still more bodies. A few had had their heads ripped off. What was the mob thinking? I asked myself. They would fare no better against the monster. Of course mobs and rational thought are not complementary. I have seen too many mobs in my day.

When we reached the trees on the edge of town, I

left the rabble to search for the monster myself. I could hear it, two miles ahead, laughing uproariously as it tore off the head of an animal. It was fast and strong, but I was a pure vampire, not a hybrid. It would be no match for me.

I came across it as it ducked from tree to tree, preparing to attack the mob.

"Ralphe," I whispered as I moved up behind him.

He whirled around, his face covered with blood, a wild light in his eyes. Or I should say, no light shone there. His eyes were snakelike. He was a serpent on the prowl, searching for the eggs of another reptile. Yet he recognized me—a faint flicker of affection crossed his face. If it was not for that, I would have killed him instantly. I had no hope he could be converted back to what he had been. I have intuition of my own. Some things I simply know. Usually the bitterest of things.

"Sita," he hissed. "Are you hungry? I am hungry."

I moved closer, not wanting to alert the mob, which was closing in. Ralphe had left a trail of blood. The stuff dripped off him; it was enough to make even me sick. My heart broke in my chest as he came within arm's reach.

"Ralphe," I said softly, all the time knowing it was hopeless. "I have to take you back to Arturo. You need help."

Terror disfigured his bloody expression. Obviously the transformation had not been pleasant for him. "I will not go back there!" he shouted. "He made me hungry!" Ralphe paused to stare down at his sticky hands. A portion of his humanity did indeed remain. His voice faltered on a lump of sorrow in his throat. "He made me do this."

"Oh, Ralphe." I took him in my arms. "I'm so sorry. This should never have happened."

"Sita," he whispered, nuzzling his face into my body. I could not kill him, I told myself. Not for the whole world. But just as I swore the vow inside, I leapt back in pain, barely stifling a cry. He had bitten me! His sorrow had vanished in a lick of his lips. I watched in horror as he chewed down a portion of my right arm, an insane grin on his face. "I like you, Sita," he said. "You taste good!"

"Would you like more?" I asked, offering him my other arm, tears filling my eyes. "You can have all you want. Come closer, Ralphe. I like you, too."

"Sita," he said lustfully as he grabbed my arm and started to take another bite. It was then I spun him around in my arms and gripped his skull from behind. With all the force I could muster and before my tears overwhelmed me, I yanked his head back and to the side. Every bone in his neck broke. His small body went limp in my arms—he had not felt any pain, I told myself.

"My Ralphe," I whispered, running my hands through his long fine hair.

I should have fled with his body then, buried it in the hills. But the execution was too much, even for a monster like me. The life went out of me and I wanted to collapse. When the mob found me, I was cradling

Ralphe's body in my arms, weeping like a common mortal. My ancient daughter, my young son—God had stolen them both from me.

The mob surrounded me.

They wanted to know how I had stopped the demon child.

A few in the mob knew me.

"You take care of this boy!" they cried. "We saw you and the priest with him!"

I could have killed them right then, all fifty of them. But the night had seen too much death. I let them drag me back to the town, their torches burning in my bleary eyes. They threw me in a dungeon near the center of town, where the executions took place, taunting me that they were going to get to the bottom of how this abomination was created. Before the sun rose, I knew they would be pounding on Arturo's door, digging into his secret underground chamber, collecting the necessary evidence to show the feared inquisitors. There would be a trial and there would be a judge. The only problem was, there could be only one sentence.

Yet I was Sita, a vampire of incomparable power. Even the hard hand of the Church could not close around my throat unless I allowed it. But what about Arturo? I loved him but could not trust him. If he lived, he would continue his experiments. It was inevitable because he believed it was his destiny. He had enough of my blood left to make another Ralphe, or worse.

A few hours later they threw him in a cell across from me. I begged him to talk to me but he refused. Huddled up in a corner, staring at the wall with eyes as vacant as dusty mirrors, he gave no indication of what was going through his mind. His God did not come to save him. That was left for me to do.

I ended up testifying against him.

The inquisitor told me it was the only way to save my life. Even chained in the middle of the high court with soldiers surrounding me, I could have broken free and destroyed them all. How tempting it was for me to reach out and rip open the throat of the evil-faced priest, who conducted his investigation like a hungry dog on a battlefield searching for fresh meat. Yet I could not kill Arturo with my own hands. It would have been impossible. But I could not have him live and continue his search for the sacred blood of Jesus Christ. Jesus had died twelve hundred years ago, and the search would never end. It was a paradox— the only solution was agonizing. I could not stop Arturo so I had to let others stop him.

"Yes," I swore on the Holy Bible. "He created the abomination. I saw him do it with my own eyes. He *changed* that boy. Then he tried to seduce me with the black arts. He is a witch, Father, that fact is indisputable. God strike me down if I lie!"

The old friar at the church also testified against Arturo, although the inquisitor had to first stretch him on the *strappado* to get the words out of his mouth. It broke the friar's heart to condemn Arturo. He was not alone in his guilt.

Arturo never confessed, no matter how much they tortured him. He was too proud, his cause too noble, in his mind. After the trial, we never spoke. Indeed, I never saw him again. I didn't attend his execution. But I heard they burned him at the stake.

Like any witch.

9

I sit at a poker table trying to bluff a high roller from Texas into folding. The game has been going on awhile. There is one hundred thousand dollars in cash and chips on the table. His hand is better than mine. Yaksha's mind-reading gift has grown more powerful in me—I can now see the man's cards as if viewing them through his eyes. He has three aces, two jacks—a full house. I have three sixes—Satan's favorite number. He has the winning hand.

The Texan wears leather cowboy boots, a five-gallon hat. The smoke from his fat cigar does not irritate my eyes. He blows a smelly cloud my way as if to intimidate me. I smile and match his last bet, then raise him another fifty thousand. We are enjoying a private game, in a luxurious corner of the casino, where only fat cats hang out. Three other men sit with us at the table, but they have since folded. They follow the action closely—they all know each other. The Texan will not like to be humiliated in front of them.

"You must have a royal flush, honey child," he says. "Betting the way you do." He leans across the table. "Or else you got a sugar daddy paying your bills."

"Honey and sugar," I muse aloud. "Both are sweet —like me." I add, sharpening my tone, "But I pay my own bills."

He laughs and slaps his leg. "Are you trying to bluff me?"

"Maybe. Match my bet and find out."

He hesitates a moment, glancing at the pot. "The action is getting kind of heavy. What do you do, child, to have so much dough? Your daddy must have given it to you."

He is trying to ascertain how important the money is to me. If it means a lot, in my mind, then I will be betting heavily only if I have an unbeatable hand. Leaning across the table, I stare him in the eye, not strong enough to fry his synapses but hard enough to shake him. I don't like being called a child. I am five thousand years old after all.

"I earned every penny of it," I tell him. "The hard way. Where did you get your money, old man?"

He sits back quickly, ruffled by my tone, my laser vision. "I earned it by honest labor," he says, lying.

I sit back as well. "Then lose it honestly. Match my bet or fold. I don't care which. Just quit stalling."

He flushes. "I'm not stalling."

I shrug, cool as ice. "Whatever you want to call it, old man."

"Damn you," he swears, throwing his cards down. "I fold."

My arms reach out and rake in the money. They're all staring at me. "Oh," I say. "I bet you're wondering what I had? But you're all too professional to ask, aren't you?" I stand and start to stuff the cash and chips in my purse. "I think I'll call it a night."

"Wait right there," the Texan says, getting up. "I want to see those cards."

"Really? I thought you had to pay to see them. Are the rules different for Texans?"

"They are when you've got fifty grand of my money, bitch. Now show me."

I dislike being called a "bitch" more than a "child."

"Very well," I say, flipping over my cards. "You would have won. That's the last time I show a hand you didn't pay to see. Now do you feel better? You were bluffed out of your wrinkled skin, old man."

He slams the table with his fist. "Who are you anyway?"

I shake my head. "You're a sore loser, and I've wasted enough time on you." I turn away. One of his partners grabs my arm. That is a mistake.

"Hold on now, honey," he says. The others move closer.

I smile. "Yes?" Of course I am protected by the casino. I need only raise my voice and these men will be thrown out. But I dislike going to others for help, when I am so capable of taking care of myself. Dinner will be a four-course meal tonight, I think. "What can I do for you?" I ask.

The man continues to hold on to my arm but doesn't respond. He glances at the Texan, who is clearly the boss. The Texan has regained his smile.

"We would just like to play some more, honey," he says. "That's only fair. We need a chance to win our money back."

My smile widens. "Why don't I just give you the money back?"

My offer confuses him. The Texan shrugs. "If you want. I'll be happy to accept it."

"Good," I say. "Meet me at the west end of the hotel parking lot in ten minutes. We'll go for a little drive. You'll get all your money back." I glance at the others. "The only condition is you must all come."

"Why do we have to go anywhere?" the Texan asks. "Just give it to us now."

I shake off the other's hold on me. "Surely you're not afraid of little old me, sugar daddy?" I say sweetly.

The men laugh together, a bit uneasily. The Texan points a finger at me.

"In ten minutes," he says. "Don't be late."

"I never am," I reply.

We meet as planned and drive a short distance from town, each in our own cars. Then I lead them off the road and into the desert a few miles, stopping near a low-lying hill. The time is eleven at night, the evening cool and clear, the almost full moon brilliant against the night sky. The men park beside me and climb out. They *are* afraid of me. I can smell their fear. Except for the big boss, they are armed. The bulges beneath their coats are noticeable. I smell the gunpowder in their bullets. They probably figure I am setting them up to be robbed. They study the terrain as they walk toward me, puzzled that I am alone. They are not very subtle. Two of them have their hands thrust in their coat pockets, their fingers wound around their handguns. The Texan steps in front and reaches out to me.

"Give us your bag," Tex orders.

"All right." I hand him my bag. The money is inside, much to his pleasure. His eyes are wide as he counts it. I know he had expected to find a gun in the bag. "Are you satisfied?" I ask.

Tex nods to a partner. I am frisked. Roughly.

"She's cool," the partner mumbles a moment later, backing away.

Tex stuffs the money in his pockets. "Yeah, I'm satisfied. But I don't get it. Why did you drag us all the way out here?"

"I'm hungry," I say.

He grins like the crooked oil baron that he is. "We would have been happy to have taken you to dinner, honey pie. We still can. What would you like?"

"Prime ribs," I say.

He slaps his leg again. Must be a nervous gesture with him. "Goddamn! That's my favorite. Ribs dripping with red juice. We'll take you out and get you some right now." He adds with a phony wink, "Then maybe we can have a little fun afterward."

I shake my head as I take a step toward him. "We can eat here. We can have a picnic. Just the five of us."

He glances at my car. "Did you bring some goodies?"

"No. You did."

His impatience is never far away. "What are you talking about?"

I throw my head back and laugh. "You're such a fake! Your politeness only appears when it is useful to you. Now that you have stolen the money I won fair and square, you want to take me out for dinner."

Tex is indignant. "We did not steal this money. You offered to return it to us."

"After pressure from you. Let's call a spade a spade. You're a crook."

"No one calls me that and gets away with it!"

"Really? What are you going to do? Kill me?"

He steps forward and slaps me across the face with the back of his hand. "Bitch! You just be happy I'm not that kind of man."

I put a hand to my mouth. "Aren't you that kind of man?" I ask softly. "I see your heart, Mr. Money Bags. You have killed before. It's good we meet tonight, out here in the desert. If you lived, you would probably kill again."

He turns to leave. "Let's get out of here, boys."

"Wait," I say. "I have something else to give you."

He glances over his shoulder. "What?"

I take another step forward. "I have to tell you who I really am. You did ask, remember?"

Tex is in a hurry. "So, who are you? A Hollywood star?"

"Close. I am famous, in certain circles. Why just a few days ago the entire LAPD was chasing me around town. You read about it in the papers?"

A wary note enters his voice. Once again, his men glance around, this time looking for Arab backups. "You're not connected to that group of terrorists, are you?"

"There were no terrorists. That was just the cops trying to cover their asses. It was just me and my partner. We caused all the ruckus."

He snorts. "Right. You and your partner wasted twenty cops. You must be a terminator, huh?"

"Close. I'm a vampire. I'm five thousand years old."

He snickers. "You're a psycho, and you're wasting my time." He turns again. "Good night."

I grab him by the back of his collar and yank him close, pressing his cheek next to mine. He is so startled—he hardly reacts. But his men are better trained. Suddenly I have three revolvers pointed at me. Quickly, I shield myself with Tex. My grip on him tightens, cutting off his air. He gags loudly.

"I am in a generous mood," I say calmly to the others. "I will give you men a chance to escape. Ordinarily I would not even consider it. But since my cover has been blown, I am not so picky about destroying every shred of evidence." I pause and catch each of their eyes, no doubt sending a shiver to the base of their spines. "I suggest you get in your cars and get out of here—out of Las Vegas completely. If you don't, you will die. It is that simple." I throttle Tex and he moans in pain. My voice takes on a mocking tone, "You can see how strong I am for a honey child."

"Shoot her," Tex gasps as I allow him a little air.

"That is a bad idea," I say. "To shoot me they have to shoot you first because you are standing in front of me. Really, Tex, you should think these things out before giving such orders." I glance at the others. "If you don't get out of here, I'll have you for dinner as well. I really am a vampire and, for me, prime ribs come in all shapes and forms." With one hand, I lift Tex two feet off the ground. "Do you want to see what I do to him? I guarantee it will make you sick to your stomach."

"God," one of the men whispers and turns to flee. He doesn't bother with the car. He just runs into the desert, anywhere to get away from me. Another fellow edges toward the periphery. But the remaining man— the guy who grabbed me in the casino, the same one who frisked me—snaps at him.

"She's not a vampire," he says. "She's just some kind of freak."

"That's it," I agree. "I take steroids." I glance at the guy who wants to leave. "Get out of here while you still can. You will see neither of these men alive again. Believe me, you'll hear their screams echoing over the desert."

My tone is persuasive. The guy leaves, chasing after

the first one. Now there are just the three of us. How cozy. In reality, I was not looking forward to having to dodge the bullets fired by three separate men. I allow Tex a little more air, let him say his last words. His tune has not changed.

"Shoot her," he croaks at his partner.

"You could try it and see what happens," I remark.

The hired hand is unsure. His gun wavers in the air. "I can't get a clear shot."

Tex tries to turn toward me. "We can make a deal. I have money."

I shake my head. "Too late. I don't want your money. I just want your blood."

Tex sees I am serious. My eyes and voice appear devilishly wicked when I am in the mood, and I'm starving right now. Tex turns deathly pale, matching the color of the moonlight that pours down on us.

"You can't kill me!" he cries.

I laugh. "Yes. It will be very easy to kill you. Do you want me to demonstrate?"

He trembles. "No!"

"I will give you a demonstration anyway." I call over to Tex's partner, who has begun to perspire heavily. "What is your name?"

"Go to hell," he swears, trying to circle around us, to get off a lucky shot.

"That cannot be your name," I say. "Your mother would never have called you that. It doesn't matter. You are going to be nobody in a minute. But before I kill you, is there anything you want to say?"

He pauses, angry. "Say to who?"

I shrug. "I don't know. God, maybe. Do you believe in God?"

I exasperate him. "You are one weird bitch."

I nod solemnly. "I am weird." The full power of my gaze locks into his eyes. With me boring into him, he is unable to look away. All he sees, I know, is my fathomless pupils, swelling in size like black holes. I speak very slowly, softly. "Now my dear man, you are going to take your gun and put it in your mouth."

The man freezes for a moment.

Then, as if in a dream, he opens his mouth and puts the gun between his lips.

"Chuck!" Tex screams. "Don't listen to her! She's trying to hypnotize you!"

"Now I want you to grasp the trigger," I continue in my penetrating voice. "I want you to place a certain amount of pressure on the trigger. Not enough to fire the bullet, mind you, but almost enough. There, that is perfect, you have done well. You are half an inch from death." I pause and turn down the power of my eyes. My voice returns to normal. "How does it feel?"

The man blinks and then notices the barrel in his mouth. He almost has a heart attack. He is so scared, he actually drops the gun. "Jesus Christ!" he cries.

"See," I say. "You must believe in God. And because I do as well, and I can only drink the blood of one of you at a time, I think I will let you go as well. Quick, join your partners out in the desert, before I change my mind."

The man nods. "No problem." He dashes away.

"Chuck!" Tex screams. "Come back here!"

"He is not coming back," I tell Tex seriously. "You cannot buy that kind of loyalty. You certainly cannot buy me. You can't even buy my dinner." I pause. "You must understand by now that you *are* dinner."

He weeps like a child. "Please! I don't want to die."

I pull him closer, whisper my favorite line.

"Then you should never have been born," I say.

I enjoy my meal.

When I am finished draining the Texan and have buried him far from his car, I go for a walk in the desert. My thirst is satisfied but my mind is restless. Andy will be off work in a few hours. I should be planning how I will convince him to help me, yet I cannot concentrate. I keep thinking I'm missing something important. I contemplate the last few days and somehow I know something is missing—a piece of the puzzle. This piece exists just beyond the edge of my vision. What it is, I cannot grasp.

Arturo's ghost haunts me. The world never knew what it had lost in him. What greater sorrow could there be? I ask myself how he would have been remembered if there had been no Inquisition. If there had been no Sita and no magical blood to poison his dreams. Perhaps his name would have been uttered in the same breath as that of Leonardo da Vinci, of Einstein. It tortures me to think of the lost possibilities. Arturo the alchemist—the founder of a secret science.

"What did you do to Ralphe?" I whisper aloud. "Why did you do it? Why did you refuse to talk to me when we were in jail?"

But his ghost has questions of its own.

Why were you so quick to kill Ralphe?

"I had to," I tell the night.

Why did you betray me, Sita?

"I had to," I say again. "You were out of control."

But I never accused you, Sita. And you were the real witch.

I sigh. "I know, Arturo. And I was not a good witch."

I have come far from where I started. A steep hill stands before me and I climb to the top of it. Twenty miles off to my left is Las Vegas, glowing with extravagance and decadence. The almost full moon is high and to my right. The hike has left me hot and sweaty. After shedding my clothes, I once more bow to the lunar goddess. This time I feel the rays enter my body, a tingling coolness that is strangely comforting. My breathing becomes deep and expanded. I feel as if my lungs can draw in the whole atmosphere, as if my skin can soak up the entire night sky. My heart pounds in my chest, now circulating a milky white substance instead of sticky red blood. Without using my eyes, I know I am becoming transparent.

I feel extraordinarily light.

As if I could fly.

The thought comes from an unknown place. It is like a hissed whisper spoken to me from the eternal abyss. Perhaps Yaksha's soul returns to grant me one final lesson.

The soles of my feet leave the top of the hill.

But I have not jumped. No.

I am floating—a few inches above the cool sand.

10

When I return to my room, I call Seymour Dorsten, my friend and personal biographer, the young man I cured of AIDS with a few drops of my blood. Seymour is my psychic twin—he often writes about what I am experiencing, without my having to tell him what it is. Lately, I've been *broadcasting* him great material. I wake him up, but as soon as he hears my voice he is instantly alert.

"I knew you'd be calling me soon," he says. "Was that you down in Los Angeles?"

"Joel and I."

He takes a moment to absorb what I am saying. "Joel is a vampire now?"

"Yes. Eddie roughed him up bad. He was dying. I had no choice."

"You've broken your vow."

"Do you need to remind me?"

"Sorry." He pauses. "Can I become a vampire?"

"You don't want the headache. Let me tell you what's been happening."

For the next ninety minutes Seymour listens while I detail everything that has occurred since just before I rescued Yaksha and battled with Eddie. I mention Tex, sleeping in his shallow grave in the desert, and my levitating in the moonlight. Seymour ponders my words for a long time.

"Well?" I ask finally. "Have you been writing about all of this already?"

He hesitates. "I was writing a story about you. In it you were an angel."

"Did I have wings?"

"You were glowing white and flying high above a ruined landscape."

"Sounds like the end of the world," I remark.

Seymour is serious. "It will be the end of the world if you don't get Joel away from these people. You think they really have another vampire in addition to Joel?"

"Yes. Andy has constructed a model of vampire DNA. He wouldn't have had time to do it after Joel was brought to him."

"How do you know what vampire DNA looks like?"

I haven't told Seymour about Arturo. The story is too painful, and besides, I don't think it applies to the situation.

"Trust me, I have experience in the matter," I reply. "Andy's model is accurate. Anyway, whether I have to rescue one or two, my dilemma is the same. I have to get in there and then I have to get three of us out."

"It sounds like your best bet is Andy. Can't you stare him in the eye and make him do what you want?"

"That can backfire. If I push too hard, I'll scramble his brain, and the others will know there's something wrong with him. But if I'm careful I can plant a few suggestions deep in his mind."

"Money is a smart angle. Offer him millions. The fact that he hates his boss doesn't hurt either."

"I agree. But, Seymour, you're supposed to tell me what I'm missing."

"Do you feel you're missing something?" he asks.

"Yes. I can't explain, but I know it's there. It's just not evident to me."

Seymour considers. "I'll tell you a couple things you won't want to hear. When you get inside the compound, you can't go straight for Joel."

"Why not?"

"You have to get to the general. You have to be able to control him."

"He might be harder to get to than Joel."

"I doubt it. Joel will be locked in a cage even you wouldn't be able to escape from. Obviously they know how strong a vampire is."

"Joel is powerful, no doubt. But he is still a child next to me. They don't know that."

"They know more than you think, Sita. You're really not looking at the whole picture. They're probably still searching Lake Mead for your body. The fact that they haven't found it tells the general that you're still alive. And for you to have survived what they put you through means that you have to be handled with *extreme* care." Seymour pauses. "The general must have figured you'll come for Joel."

"You sound so certain," I say. "I'm not."

"Look at it logically. You had several chances to leave Joel during your fight with the LAPD—but you didn't. In fact, you showed tremendous loyalty to him. Believe me, they have constructed a psychological profile on you. They know you're coming for him. They'll be waiting for you. That's one of the reasons you have to go after the general first. Control him and his mind and you control the compound."

"His associates will know something is up."

"You need only control him for a short time. Also, you have no choice. You need the general for something other than rescue and escape."

"What?" I ask, knowing what he'll say.

"Samples of vampire blood will be spread all over the compound. I bet they have several labs there, and you won't be able to walk around and find all the samples. On top of that, they'll have the research that they've conducted in their computers. For these reasons the compound has to be completely destroyed. It's the only way. You're going to have to force the general to detonate a nuclear warhead."

"Just like that? Blow up all those people?"

"You killed plenty of people down in L.A."

My voice is cool. "I didn't enjoy that, Seymour."

He pauses. "I'm sorry, Sita. I didn't mean to imply

that you did. And I don't mean to sound cold and cruel. I'm not, you know. I'm just a high school kid, and a lousy writer on top of that."

"You're too brilliant to be lousy at anything. Please continue with your analysis. How can I get Joel out alive and blow the place up?"

He hesitates. "You might not be able to do both."

I nod to myself. "This could be a suicide mission. I've thought of that." I add sadly, "Won't you miss me?"

He speaks with feeling. "Yes. Come here tonight. Make me a vampire. I'll help you."

"You're not vampire material."

"Why? I'm not sexy enough?"

"Oh, that's not the problem. If you were a vampire, I'm sure you'd be a sex machine. It's just that you're too special to be . . ." My voice falters as I think of Arturo. "To be contaminated by my blood."

"Sita? What's wrong?"

I swallow past my pain. "It's nothing—the past. That's the trouble with living for five thousand years—I have so much past. It's hard to live in the present when all that history is inside you."

"Your blood saved my life," Seymour says gently.

"How are you feeling? Are the HIV tests still negative?"

"Yes, I'm fine. Don't worry about me. When do you see Andy next?"

"In a few hours, near dawn. Then, when he returns to work in the evening, I plan to stow away in the trunk of his car."

"You'll need his cooperation. You can't go searching the compound for Joel."

"Andy will cooperate, one way or the other." I pause. "Is there anything else you can tell me that might help?"

"Yeah. Practice that levitating trick. You never know when it'll come in handy."

"I don't know what's causing it."

"Obviously, Yaksha's blood. He must have developed the ability over the centuries. Could he fly when you knew him in India?"

"He never demonstrated that he could."

"You vampires are full of surprises."

I sigh. "You're so anxious to become like me. You envy my powers. But what you don't know is that I envy you more."

Seymour is surprised. "What do I have that you could possibly want?"

I think of Lalita, my daughter.

But I cannot talk about children, on this of all nights.

"You're human" is all I say.

11

When Andy gets to my suite, he acts stressed out but excited. He is in the door only a minute when I give him a hard kiss on the lips. He wants more, and reaches for it, but I push him away.

"Later," I whisper. "The night is still young."

"It's almost morning," he says, recalling my line from the night before.

I turn away. "I want to gamble first."

For a degenerate gambler, I know, dice are better than sex.

"Now you're talking, Lara," he says.

We go down to the casino. It's only a few days before Christmas but the place is packed. The image of a nuclear bomb exploding on the Strip haunts me. Of course, that will never happen. Even if we set a nuclear warhead to go off at the compound, it would not affect Las Vegas, except for slight fallout—if the wind is blowing the wrong way. I wonder if Seymour's dream means I will succeed in my mission or fail.

A glowing angel, flying above the world?

We play craps, dice, and I am the designated roller. Without trying, I throw ten passes in a row and the table cheers me on. Andy bets heavily, wins plenty, and drinks even more. Before we leave the first table, he is drunk. I scold him.

"How can you be a scientist when you keep killing off your brain cells?" I ask.

He laughs, throwing an arm over my shoulder. "I'd rather be a lover than a scientist."

We walk down the Strip to another casino, the Excalibur. Here it is even more crowded. It is a fact that the town never sleeps. We play blackjack, twenty-one. I count cards, only betting heavily when the deck favors the player. But the advantage from even perfect counting is limited, and we don't win any money. Andy drags me back to the dice table—his favorite. The dice come to me, and again I throw another six passes in a row. But I don't want Andy to win too much and be free of debt. Just as the sun begins to color the sky, I drag him back to the Mirage, to my hotel suite. Once there, he falls on my bed, exhausted.

"I hate what I do," he mutters to the ceiling.

I hate that I can't read his mind. It must be the booze. I sit beside him. "Another hard night at work?"

"I shouldn't talk about it."

"You can. Don't worry—I'm good at keeping secrets."

"My boss is crazy."

"The general?"

"Yes. He's stark raving mad."

"What do you mean? What is he doing?"

Andy sits up and glances at me with bloodshot eyes. "Remember I told you we were working on an amazing discovery?"

"Yes. You said it was one of the greatest discoveries of modern time." I smile. "I thought you were trying to impress me."

He shakes his head. "I wasn't exaggerating. We're playing with explosive genetic material, and that's putting it mildly. This general has ordered us to artifically clone it. Do you know what that means?"

I nod. "You're going to make more of it—in a test tube."

"Yes. That's a layman's view, but it is essentially correct." He stares out the window, at the glitter that is the Strip. When he speaks again, his voice reflects the horror he feels. "We are going to try to duplicate something that, if it got out, could affect all of mankind."

It's worse than I thought. The charade must end.

He has given me an opening. I must seize it.

"Andy?" I whisper.

He looks at me. I catch his eye.

"Yes, Lara?" he says.

I do not push him, not yet, but I do not let him turn

away either. A narrow tunnel of whirling blue fog exists between us. He is at one end, chained to a hard wall, and I am steadily rushing toward him, shadows at my back. I hold his attention but slightly blur his focus. Since ingesting Yaksha's blood, my mind-altering abilities are more refined, more powerful. I have to be careful I don't destroy his brain.

"My name is not Lara."

He tries to blink, fails. "What is it?"

"It doesn't matter. I am not who I appear to be." I pause. "I know what you are working on."

He hesitates. "How?"

"I know your prisoner. He is a friend of mine."

"No."

"Yes. I lied to you last night, and I'm sorry. I won't lie to you anymore. I came to Las Vegas for the purpose of freeing my friend." I touch his knee. "But I didn't come to hurt you. I didn't know I would end up caring for you."

He has to take a breath. "I don't understand what you're saying?"

I have to relax my hold on him. The pressure inside his skull is building. Sweat stands out on his forehead. Standing, I turn my back to him and walk to the window to look out at the Strip. The Christmas decorations glitter even amid the neon in the faint light of the dawn.

"But you do understand," I say. "You are holding a prisoner, Joel Drake. He is an FBI agent, but since you have begun to examine him you have come to see that he's much more than that. His blood is different from that of most humans, and this difference makes him very strong, very quick. That's why you keep him locked up in a special cell. Your general tells you he is dangerous. Yet this same general makes you and your partners work night and day so that you can change more people's blood to match that of the supposedly dangerous prisoner." I pause. "Is this not accurate, Andy?"

He is a long time answering. His voice comes out hesitantly.

"How do you know these things?"

I turn to face him. "I told you. I am his friend. I am here to rescue him. I need your help."

Andy can't stop staring at me. It's as if I'm a ghost.

"They said there was another," he mumbles.

"Yes."

"Are you the one?"

"Yes."

He winces. "Are you like him?"

"Yes."

He puts a hand to his head. "Oh God."

Once more, I sit beside him on the bed.

"We are not evil," I say. "I know what you must have been told, but it is not true. We only fight when threatened. The men and woman who died in L.A. trying to arrest us—we didn't want to harm them. But they came after us, they cornered us. We had no choice but to defend ourselves."

His head is buried in his hands. He is close to weeping. "But you killed many others before that night."

"That is not true. The one who did the killing—he was an aberration. His name was Eddie Fender. He accidentally got ahold of our blood. I stopped him, but Eddie is a perfect example of what can happen if this blood gets out. You said it yourself a moment ago—it could affect all of humanity. Worse, it would destroy all of humanity. I am here to stop that. I am here to help you."

He peers up at me, his fingers still covering much of his face. "That's why you can throw the dice the way you do?"

"Yes."

"What else can you do?"

I shake my head. "It doesn't matter. All that matters is that more people are not allowed to become like me and my friend."

"How many are there of you?" he asks.

"I thought there were just two of us left. But I suspect you have another at the compound." I pause. "Do you?"

He turns away. "I can't tell you. I don't know who you are."

"Yes, you know me better than anyone. You've seen what my DNA is like."

He stands and walks to the far wall. He puts a hand on it for support, breathing rapidly. "The man you speak of—Joel—he's ill. He has fever, severe cramps. We don't know what to do with him." Andy struggles. My revelation is too much for him. "Do you know?" he asks.

"Yes. Have you kept him out of the sunlight?"

"Yes. He's in a cell, in a basement. There is no sun." He pauses. "Is he allergic to the sun?"

"Yes."

Andy frowns. "But how does it make him ill? I told you, he doesn't see it."

"The sun is not what makes him ill. I was only ruling out a possibility. He is sick because he is hungry."

"But we have fed him. It doesn't help."

"You are not feeding him what he needs."

"What is that?"

"Blood."

Andy almost crumbles. "No," he moans. "You're like vampires."

I stand and approach him cautiously, not wishing to scare him worse than I already have. "We *are* vampires, Andy. Joel has been one only a few days. I changed him in order to prevent him from dying. Eddie had mortally wounded him. Believe me, I don't go around making vampires. It's against my— principles."

Andy struggles to get a grip on himself. "Who made you?"

"A vampire by the name of Yaksha. He was the first of our kind."

"When was this?"

"A long time ago."

"When?" he demands.

"Five thousand years ago."

My revealing my age does not help the situation. The strength goes out of Andy; he slides to the floor.

Rolling into a ball, he recoils as I come closer. I halt in midstride.

"What do you want from me?" he mumbles.

"Your help. I need to get into your compound and get my friend out before the world is destroyed. It is that simple. The danger is that great. And you know I'm not exaggerating. Our blood in the hands of your general is more dangerous than plutonium in the hands of terrorists."

Andy nods weakly. "Oh, I believe that."

"Then you will help me?"

My question startles him. "What? How can I help you? You're some kind of monster. You're the source of this danger."

I speak firmly. "I have walked this world since the dawn of history. In all that time, there have been only myths and rumors of my existence, and the existence of others like me. And those myths and rumors weren't based on fact. They were just stories. Because in all this time none of us has set out to destroy humanity. Yet your general will do this, whether he wants to or not. Listen to me, Andy! He has to be stopped and you have to help me stop him."

"No."

"Yes! Do you want him to clone Joel's blood? Do you want that material shipped to a weapons plant in the heart of the Pentagon?"

Anger shakes Andy. "No! I want to destroy the blood! I don't need your lectures. I know what it can do. I have studied it inside out."

I move closer, kneel on the floor beside him. "Look at me, Andy."

He lowers his head. "You might cast a spell on me."

"I don't need spells to convince you of the truth. I am not the enemy. Without my assistance, you won't be able to stop this thing from progressing to the next level. Try to imagine a society where everyone has our vampire strength and appetites."

The visions I conjure make him sick. "You really drink human blood?"

"Yes. I need it to live. But I do not need to kill or even harm the person I drink from. Usually, they don't even know what has happened. They just wake up the next day with a headache."

My remark causes him to smile unexpectedly. "I woke up with a headache this evening. Did you drink some of my blood without my knowing?"

I chuckle softly. "No. Your headaches are your problem. Unless you cut down on the booze, your liver is going to give out. Listen to the advice of a five-thousand-year-old doctor."

He finally looks at me. "You're not really that old, are you?"

"I was alive when Krishna walked the earth. I met him in fact."

"What was he like?"

"Cool."

"Krishna was cool?"

"Yes. He didn't kill me. He mustn't have thought I was a monster."

Andy is calming down. "I'm sorry I called you that. It's just—well, I've never met a vampire before. I mean, I was never in a hotel room with one."

"Aren't you glad you didn't sleep with me last night?"

He obviously forgot that small point. "Would I have been changed into a vampire?"

"It takes more than sex with an immortal to make you immortal." I speak delicately. "But you may know that."

He is grim. "There has to be a blood transfer to bring about the change. I imagine a lot of blood is involved."

"Yes, that is correct. Have your experiments established that?"

"We have established a few things. But the human immune system reacts violently to this kind of blood. It embraces it and at the same time tries to destroy it. We have postulated that a large infusion of this DNA code would transform the entire system. Actually, we think your DNA would just take over, and replicate itself throughout every cell in the body." He pauses. "Is that what happened when *Yaksha* changed you?"

I hesitate. I don't want to give him information that could be used later.

"When he changed me, I was young. I cried through most of it."

"He is dead now?"

"Yes."

"When did he die?"

"A few days ago." I add, "He wanted to die."

"Why?"

I smile faintly, sadly. "He wanted to be with Krishna. That was all that mattered to him. He was evil when he changed me. But when he died—he was a saint. He loved God very much."

Andy stares at me, mystified. "You're telling me the truth."

I nod weakly. The thought of Krishna always shakes me.

"Yes. Maybe I should have told you from the beginning. You see, I was going to try to hypnotize you. I was going to seduce you and offer you money and set your head spinning—until you didn't know what you were doing." I touch his leg gently. "But none of that is necessary now. You are a true scientist. You seek the truth. You don't want to harm people. And you know that this blood can harm many people. Give it back to me. I know how to care for it, to keep it out of harm's way."

"If I help you into the compound, they will lock me away for the rest of my life."

"Vehicles go in and out of the compound all day. I've observed them from a distance. You can bring me inside in your trunk. When no one is looking, I will climb out, and no one will blame you."

Andy's not convinced. "Your friend is in a cell in the basement of our main lab. The walls of the cell are made of a special metal alloy—even you couldn't break through. I know for a fact your partner can't. I've watched him try. Also, your friend is under constant surveillance. Cameras watch him twenty-four hours a day. Then, there is the security of the camp itself. It is surrounded by towers. The soldiers inside these towers are well armed. The place is a fortress. There are tanks and missiles behind every building." He pauses. "You won't be able to break him out."

"This special cell where Joel is being held—how does the door to it open?"

"There is a button on a control panel just outside the cell. Push it and the door swings aside. But it is a long way from my car trunk to that button. It is a longer way back outside the compound. To escape with your friend, you'll have to become invisible."

I nod. "We can go over, point by point, the security of the camp. But for now, answer my earlier question. Is there another vampire in the place?"

He hesitates, lowers his head. "Yes."

"How long has he been there? A month?"

"Yes."

"Was he captured in Los Angeles?"

"Yes. He's a black youth. He lived in South Central L.A. before he was changed." Andy looks up. "But he never said anything about an Eddie. The person who changed him was someone else. I forget the name right now."

My theory was correct. "That other person was changed by Eddie. Trust me—I know the ultimate source of this other vampire. Where is he located in relation to Joel?"

"In the cell beside Joel's. But he's virtually comatose. He has the same disease as your friend—cramps and fever." Andy shakes his head. "We didn't know what to do for him. He never asked for blood."

"Your people must have captured him right after he was changed. No one told him what he is now." It isn't pleasant to contemplate the pain this poor soul is going through. "I'll have to take him out as well."

"You'll have to carry him then."

"I can do that, if I have to."

Andy studies me. "You say you are so old. That must mean you're smarter than we short-lived mortals. If you are, you must know how the odds are stacked against you."

"I have always managed to beat the odds. Look how well I do at the dice tables."

"You will probably die if you do this."

"I'm not afraid to die."

He is impressed. "You really aren't a monster. You're much braver than I am."

I take his hand. "I was wrong a minute ago when I said your helping me would not put you at risk. It will take a brave man to sneak me inside the compound in the trunk of his car."

He squeezes my hand. "What's your real name?"

"Sita." I add, "Few people have known me by that name."

He touches my red hair. "I was wrong only to say your blood scares me. It fascinates me as well." He pauses and a sly grin crosses his face. "Sex is not enough to make me immortal?"

"It hasn't worked in the past. But these days are filled with mysterious portents." An unexpected warmth for him flows over me. His eyes—they have *me* hypnotized, with their uncanny depth, their gentle kindness. Smiling, I lean over and hug him and whisper in his ear, "The dawn is at hand. In ancient times, it was considered a time of transformation, of alchemy. I'll stay with you, for now." I pause. "Who knows what may happen?"

12 ~

I dream a dream I've had before. A dream that seems to go on forever. It takes place in eternity, at least, my idea of such a place.

I stand on a vast grassy plain with a few gently sloping hills in the far distance. It is night, yet the sky is bright. There is no sun, but a hundred blue stars blaze overhead, shimmering in a long nebulous river. The place feels familiar to me. The air is warm, saturated with sweet aromas. Miles away a large number of people walk into a vessel—a violet-colored spaceship of gigantic proportions. The vessel shines from the inside with divine radiance, almost blinding in its brilliance. I know it is about to depart and that I am supposed to be on it. Yet I cannot leave until I have finished speaking with Lord Krishna.

He stands beside me on the wide plain, his gold flute in his right hand, a red lotus flower in his left. We both have on long blue gowns. He wears an exquisite jewel around his neck—the Kaustubha gem, in which the destiny of every soul can be seen. He stares up at the sky, waiting for me to speak. But I can not remember what we were discussing.

"My Lord," I whisper. "I feel lost."

His eyes remain fixed on the stars. "You feel separate from me."

"Yes. I don't want to leave you. I don't want to go to earth."

"No. You misunderstand. You are not lost. The entire creation belongs to me—it is a part of me. How can you be lost? Your feeling of separation gives rise to your confusion." He glances my way, finally, his long black hair blowing in the soft wind. The stars shimmer in the depths of his dark eyes. The entire creation *is* there. His smile is kind, the feeling of love that pours from him overwhelming. "You have already been to earth. You are home now."

"Is this possible?" I whisper, straining to remember. Faint recollections of being on earth come to me. I recall a husband, a daughter—I can see her smile. Yet a dark film covers them. I view them from a peculiar perspective, from a mind I can scarcely believe is connected to me. In front of them many centuries stretch out, choked with endless days and nights, suffering people, all awash in blood. Blood that I have spilled. I have to force the question from my lips. "What did I do on earth, my Lord?"

"You wanted to be different—you were different. It doesn't matter. This creation is a stage, and we all play roles as heroes and villains alike. It is all *maya*—illusion."

"But did I—sin?"

My question amuses him. "It is not possible."

I glance toward the waiting vessel. It is almost full. "Then I don't have to leave you?"

He laughs. "Sita. You have not heard me. You cannot leave me. I am always with you, even when you think you are on earth." He changes his tone—he becomes more of a friend than a master. "Would you like to hear a story?"

I have to smile, although I am more confused than ever.

"Yes, my Lord," I say.

He considers. "There was once a fisherman and his wife, who lived in a small town by the ocean. Every day the fisherman would go out to sea in his boat, and his wife would stay behind and care for the house. Their life was simple, but happy. They loved each other very much.

"The wife had only one complaint about her husband—he would eat only fish. For breakfast, lunch, and dinner, he would eat only what he caught. It didn't matter what she cooked and baked: bread or pastries, rice or potatoes—he would have none of it. Fish was his food, he said, and that was the way it had to be. From an early age, he had been this way, he had taken a vow his wife could not understand.

"It came to pass one day that his wife finally got fed

up with his limited diet. She decided to trick him, to mix a piece of cooked lamb in with his fish. She did this cleverly, so that from the outside the fish looked as if it had come straight from the sea. But hidden beneath the scales of the fish was the red meat. When he returned home that evening and sat down at the table, the fish was waiting for him.

"At first he ate his meal with great relish, noticing nothing amiss. His wife sat beside him, eating the same food. But when he was halfway through, he began to cough and choke. He couldn't catch his breath. It was only then he smelled something odd on his plate. He turned to his wife, eyes blazing with anger.

"'What have you done?' he demanded. 'What is in this fish?'

"The wife sat back, scared. 'Only a little lamb. I thought you might enjoy the change.'

"At these words the fisherman wiped the plate from the table and onto the floor. His anger knew no bounds. Still, he could not catch his breath. It was as if the lamb had caught in his windpipe and refused to shake loose.

"'You've poisoned me!' he cried. 'My own wife has poisoned me!'

"'No! I only wanted to feed you something different.' She stood and slapped him on the back, but it did not help. 'Why are you choking like this?'

"The fisherman fell onto the floor, turning blue.

'Don't you know?' he gasped. 'Don't you know who I am?'

"'You are my husband,' the wife cried, kneeling beside him.

"'I am . . .' the fisherman whispered. 'I am what I am.'

"Those were his last words. The fisherman died, and as he did, his body changed. His legs turned into a large flipper. His skin became covered with silver scales. His face bulged out and his eyes became blank and cold. Because, you see, he was not a person. He was a fish, which is what he had been all along. As a big fish, he could eat only smaller fish. Everything else was poison to him." Krishna paused. "Do you understand, Sita?"

"No, my Lord."

"It doesn't matter. You are what you are. I am what I am. We are the same—when you take the time to remember me." Krishna raises his flute to his lips. "Would you like to hear a song?"

"Very much, my Lord."

"Close your eyes, listen closely. The song is always the same, Sita. But it is always changing, too. That is the mystery, that is the paradox. The truth is always simpler than you can imagine."

I close my eyes and Lord Krishna begins to play his magical flute. For a time, outside of time, that is all that matters. The music of his enchanted notes floats on a wind that blows from the heart of the galaxy. Overhead the stars shine down on us as the universe slowly revolves and the ages pass. I do not need to see my Lord to know that he is present everywhere. I do not need to touch him to feel his hand on my heart. I do not need anything, except his love. After a while, that is all there is—his divine love pouring through the center of my divine being. Truly, we are one and the same.

13 ～

I lie flat on my back in the trunk of Andy's car. My hearing is acute—up ahead I hear the noises of the compound, the guards talking at the gate. The blackness in the trunk is not totally dark to me. I clearly see the white lab coat I have donned, the fake security badge pinned to my breast pocket. The badge is an old one of Andy's. I have cleverly put my picture over his, and changed the name. I am Lieutenant Lara Adams, Ph.D., a microbiologist on loan from the Pentagon. Andy says a large number of scientists have arrived from Back East. My makeup makes me look older. I should be able to blend in.

We stop at the security gate. I hear Andy speak to the guards.

"Another long night, Harry?" Andy asks.

"Looks like it," the guard replies. "Are you working till dawn?"

"Close. This night shift is a bear—I don't know whether I'm coming or going." Andy hands something to the guard, a pass that must be electronically scanned. He has to have one to leave the compound as well. I have one in my back pocket. Andy continues in a natural voice, "I just wish I could do a little better at the tables, and quit this stupid job."

"I hear you," the guard says. "How's your luck been holding out?"

"I won a couple of grand last night."

The guard laughs. "Yeah, but how much did you lose?"

Andy laughs with him. "Three grand!"

The guard hands the pass back. "Have a good night. Don't piss off the man."

I hear Andy nod. "It's a little late for that."

We drive into the compound. Andy has promised he'll park between two sheds, out of sight of the manned towers. From my earlier examination of the place, I am familiar with the spot. As the car moves, I feel confident we are heading straight for it. Especially when Andy turns to the left, stops, and turns off the engine. He climbs out of his car, shutting the door behind him, and walks away. I listen to his steps as he enters the main lab. So far so good.

I pop open the trunk and carefully peer out.

The car sits in shadow. No one is around. After slipping out of the car, I silently close the trunk. I smooth my lab coat over my slim body, adjust my red hair. My thick glasses make me look almost nerdy but smart.

"Lara Adams from Back East," I whisper. *Back East* means the Pentagon, Andy said. They never called the place by name.

"You have to get to the general. You have to control him."

Seymour's advice remains with me. Resisting the temptation to follow Andy into the main lab—where I know Joel is being held captive—I turn instead in the direction of a small house located behind the lab. This is the general's private quarters. I move onto his front steps, then pause. I don't press the doorbell; I know without knocking that there is no one at home. Andy warned me of this. In fact, he said the general was seldom at home. Andy wants me to get Joel and get the hell out of the place, as quickly as I can. He doesn't, of course, know I need to control the general in order to blow the place up. But I have warned him that when the fireworks start, he should get out of the compound as quickly as possible.

For a moment, I stand undecided.

"The general knows you'll come for Joel."

Seymour is wise, but I still think he overestimates the intelligence of the man. For example, I tell myself, look how easily I entered the compound. The general couldn't know that I was on my way. Certainly, I can't search the entire compound for him.

I decide to have a peek at Joel. After seeing exactly

where he is, I'll be in a better position to figure out what to do next. I head back to the front entrance of the lab, where Andy disappeared.

The interior of the lab is a complex maze of halls and offices. It seems clear the real work of dissecting and analyzing is done downstairs. Men and women in lab coats mill about. There is an occasional armed soldier. No one pays any attention to me. Listening for an elevator, I hear the sound of people going up and down steps. I prefer a stairway to an elevator. The latter can be a death trap for an invading vampire.

I find the stairs and go down a couple of flights. Andy told me Joel is being held two stories below the surface, and that his cell is at the east end of the building, farthest from the main gate. On this lower floor there are fewer people. They speak in soft tones. Moving like the sharp professional I'm supposed to be, I make my way down a narrow hall toward the rear of the building. Faintly, I smell Joel's scent. But I cannot hear his heart beating, his breathing. The walls of his cell must be thick. The scent is my compass and I follow it carefully, sensitive to the way it is spread by the ventilation ducts, the passage of people.

I come to a security center, equipped with monitors and two armed soldiers. I hear everything inside the closed room. Cracking the door, I peer inside and see Joel on one of the screens. He sits in the corner of a brightly lit cage, pinned to the corner by a metallic wrist chain.

I do not see another vampire on a separate monitor. Odd.

I close the door and knock. One of the guards answers.

"Yes? Can I help you?"

"Yes. My name is Dr. Lara Adams." I nod to Joel on the screen. "I am here to talk to our patient."

The guard glances at his buddy, back to me. "You mean, over the speaker, right?"

"I would prefer to talk to him in person," I say.

The guard shakes his head. "I don't know what you've been told, but no one talks to the—to the patient directly. Only over the speaker." He pauses, glances at my badge, my breasts. Boys will be boys. "Who gave you clearance to interview this guy?"

"General Havor."

The guy raises an eyebrow. "He told you himself?"

"Yes. You can check with him if you like." I nod to the interior of the room. "May I come in?"

"Yes." The guard stands aside. "What did you say your name was?"

"Dr. Lara Adams." I gesture to the monitor. "I see this guy but where is he really? Nearby?"

"He's just around the corner," the other guard answers, while his buddy reaches for the phone. "He's in a box so thick an atomic bomb couldn't blast through it."

"Oh," I say. That is useful information.

My hands lash out, my fingers cutting the air like knives.

Both guards crumple on the floor, unconscious, not dead.

I hang up the phone. Around the corner I go.

I push the large red button to open the cage.

There is a hiss of air. A door as thick as a man's body swings aside.

"Joel," I cry softly, seeing him huddled in the corner, chained to the wall, burning like a dying coal as he shakes. I rush toward him. "I'm going to get you out of here."

"Sita," he gasps. "Don't!"

The door slams shut at my back. Locking me in.

Overhead, a TV monitor comes to life.

Andy stares down at me. Behind him stands the cruel-faced General Havor, wearing a barely disguised smirk. Yet there is no joy in Andy's expression as he slowly shakes his head and sighs. It is strange, but it is only then that I see my adversary clearly. The many years have reshapen his face, dulled his eyes, bruised his soft voice. Yet it is no excuse, not for a vampire as supposedly careful as I am. Right from the start I should have known who it was I was dealing with.

"Sita," he says sadly with a faint Italian accent. *"E'passato tanto tempo dall' Inquisizione."*

"Sita. It's been a long time since the Inquisition."

In a single horrifying instant, I understand everything.

"Arturo," I whisper.

14 ～

Several hours have elapsed since my capture. I have spent the majority of it sitting on the floor with my eyes closed, like a meditating yogi. But I enjoy no blissful nirvana. Inside, I seethe with rage: at General Havor, at Arturo, and most of all at myself. Arturo left signs for me everywhere, and I missed them all. Again and again my mind forces me to review the list.

1. When Joel was captured, he was brought before Andy. It was Andy who confirmed the special nature of Joel to General Havor. But rather than stay to examine Joel, Andy left the compound and went gambling. What an odd thing to do right after the catch of the century! Of course Andy was not out for fun. He knew I

would be watching. He knew I could be lured in.

2. I never saw Andy out in the sun, and it wasn't just because he worked the night shift. He was sensitive to the sun as a vampire should be. Yet he is not a pure vampire.

3. Andy talked about his highly classified work— to me, a total stranger. I hardly had to prod it out of him. He planted all the right clues for a person dissatisfied with his job—not enough pay, a totalitarian boss, a lousy work schedule. He tricked me in the most insidious way—by handing me all the ammunition I needed to think I could trick him.

4. He protested when I asked him to help me break into the compound. He put on a great show of defiance. But the fact that he helped me at all, without my having to manipulate his brain, was peculiar.

5. Andy had Arturo's model of vampire DNA. I passed it off, figuring he had already examined another vampire and broken the genetic code. The only problem was—there was no other vampire. I had destroyed all of Eddie's bastards. The only one the government had was Joel.

"Because, you see, he was not a person. He was a fish, which is what he had been all along. As a big fish, he could eat only smaller fish."

In my dream, Krishna had been trying to tell me that the hidden truth was the most obvious truth.

Andy was able to construct Arturo's model because he was Arturo!

Why did he leave it out for me to see? To taunt me, no doubt.

I open my eyes. "Damn," I whisper.

Joel looks over. I have broken his chains; he is no longer pinned to the wall, but is able to lie down properly and rest. The chains have accomplished their purpose, however. Had Joel been at the door, I would not have walked into the cage. I have tested the strength of the walls. The guard was right—a nuclear bomb couldn't blast through them.

The walls of the cell are a flat white color, metallic. The space is square—twenty feet by twenty feet. A seatless toilet is attached to one wall, a single cot to the opposite one. Joel lies on the thin mattress.

"We all make mistakes," he says.

"Some make more than others."

"I appreciate your trying to rescue me. You should have left me to die after Eddie opened my veins."

"You're probably right. But then I wouldn't have the pleasure of your company right now." I pause. "How are you feeling?"

The first thing I did after being captured, before sitting down to berate myself, was let Joel drink a pint of my blood. The transfusion alleviated his more severe symptoms but he still looked gaunt. Yet I am reluctant to give him more nourishment. We both know I need to be at full strength if we are to break out.

"I feel fine." He adds, "Better than I have in days."

I reach out and squeeze his hand. "It must have been hard for you. Have they been examining you inside out?"

"That's a literal way of putting the question." He gestures to the screen. I have told him nothing of Arturo. "I take it he is an old friend?"

I know our every word is being recorded. I don't know what can and will be used against me in a court of law. But I do know I don't have the right to remain silent. I wonder if they will try to torture information out of me. It will be a waste of their time. I doubt they're going to let me call a lawyer.

"We go way back" is all I say.

"How was Vegas?"

"Fine. Won a lot of money at craps."

"That's great. Where did you stay?"

"At the Mirage." I sigh. "I'm sorry, Joel. Neither of us should be in here. I messed up."

"Don't be so hard on yourself. After all, you stopped Eddie."

"Yeah. Only to set up a situation where there might be a thousand Eddies." I abruptly raise my voice and yell at the monitor. "Did you hear that, Arturo? A thousand Ralphes running loose! Is that what you want?" My voice sinks to a whisper. "That's what you're going to get."

I don't expect to get a response to my outburst, but a minute later the TV monitor comes back to life.

Arturo is alone, sitting at a desk in the security room. Around the corner, as they say.

"Sita," he says. *"None oho mai pensato che ti avrei rivista."*

"I never thought I would see you again."

"Same here," I mutter.

"Are you comfortable?" he asks, switching languages effortlessly. When he wishes, he has no accent. He must have been living in America for a long time.

"No cage is ever comfortable." I pause. "Are you comfortable?"

He spreads his hands. I remember how large they were. Suddenly, I recall many details about him: the warm gray of his eyes, the strength of his jawline. Why didn't I recognize him? There are the obvious reasons. He has aged twenty-five years since we last met, and yet, his face has changed more than the two and a half decades warrant. Probably since it has, in reality, been over seven hundred years.

Yet none of that should have fooled me. I didn't recognize him for two sound reasons: I knew he couldn't possibly exist in our time, so I never even considered the idea; and the Andy I stalked did not possess the same soul as the Arturo I once loved. This man who stares down at me—I hardly know him, and I slept with him for months.

"What would you have me do?" he replies. "You had to be stopped."

My voice is filled with scorn. "Stopped from what?"

"There were the violent murders in Los Angeles. I knew that was you."

"You knew it was not me! You knew it was some other vampire! Don't start off our first conversation in seven centuries with a lie. You know I never killed for pleasure."

My wrath makes him pull back a step. "I apologize. I should say I knew you were indirectly involved." He pauses. "Who committed the killings?"

I forget my resolve to say as little as possible. The information cannot help them, anyway. My blood is all that matters.

"A psychotic vampire by the name of Eddie Fender started the murders. The LAPD and the FBI were doing everything they could to stop him. But it was I who put a halt to the killings. And what do I get for it? A medal? No, the entire police force comes after me."

"You killed two dozen of those officers."

"Because they were trying to kill me! I am not the villain here. You and the scum you are associated with are." I pause, settle down. "Why are you with these people?"

"I can help them. They can help me. We have vested interests. Isn't that the reason for most partnerships?"

"It is among people who have selfish goals. But I never remember you as selfish. Why are you working for the U.S. military machine?"

"Surely you must understand by now. I need to complete my experiments."

I laugh. "Are you still searching for the blood of Christ?"

"You say it as if it were a fool's errand."

"It's a blasphemous errand. You saw what happened last time."

"I made an error—that's all. I will not make the same error again."

"That's all? Just some error? What about Ralphe? I loved that boy. You loved him. And you turned him into a monster. You forced me to kill him. Do you know what that did to me?"

Arturo's voice goes cold. "It made you want to testify against me?"

"You had to be stopped. I didn't have the strength or the will to do it myself." I pause. "You had a chance to talk to me in the inquisitor's dungeon. You chose not to."

"I had nothing to say."

"Well, then, I have nothing to say to you now. Come, get your fresh supply of vampire blood. Send plenty of scientists and soldiers. Not all of them will be coming back to you."

"You present no danger to us as long as you are in your cell. And you will remain in there for the remainder of your life."

"We will see," I whisper faintly.

"Sita, I'm surprised at you. Aren't you curious how I'm still alive?"

I draw in a weary breath. "I have an idea as to how you survived. Even when you swore to me you weren't experimenting on yourself, you were. That's why you began to have visions of DNA. You were seeing it through the eyes of your blessed hybrid state."

"I did experiment on myself. That is true. But I never reached the full hybrid status. That must be obvious to you."

I nod. "Because you have aged. Does it hurt, Arturo, that you're not the dashing young priest anymore?"

"I may yet achieve immortality."

"Hmm. And I always thought you wanted to die and go to heaven." He is right, of course; I am curious about those days. "What happened after the trial? How did you escape? I heard they burned you at the stake."

"The inquisitor granted me a private audience. He couldn't let me go, he said, but in exchange for my confession of witchcraft, he agreed to hang instead of burn me."

"And you recovered?"

"Yes."

"Were you surprised?"

"Yes. It was a calculated risk. I didn't have many options."

I hesitate. "What did you do to Ralphe?"

For once, Arturo looks ashamed. "I exposed him to the vial of your blood—with the midday sun pouring through it."

I was aghast. "But you said you'd never consider that. The vibration would destroy a man or woman."

"You saw how the word was spreading about me. I had only a limited time to complete my experiments. Ralphe had been spying on us all along. Neither of us knew. He saw what we were up to. He wanted to try it."

Fury possesses me. "That's a ridiculous rationalization! He was a child! He didn't know what would happen to him! You did!"

"Sita."

"You were a coward! If your experiment was so precious to you, why didn't you perform it on yourself, with the midday sun pouring through my bloody vial?"

My words wound him, but he is still full of surprises. "But I did subject myself to the blood in the sunlight. That morning, when the mob approached the church, I heard them coming. I hurried down to the basement and let the full power of the vampire vibration wash over me. I believe that is why I have been able to live as long as I have. If the mob had not stopped me, maybe the transformation would have been complete, and I would have achieved the perfect state. I was never to know. The first thing the mob did was break the vial."

His words sober me. "Then what went wrong with Ralphe? Why did he turn into a monster?"

"There could be many factors that influenced his outcome. One was that I laid him on the copper sheets when the sun was high in the sky. Also—and I think this is the primary reason the experiment failed—Ralphe was ordinarily fearless by nature. But when the transformation started, he got scared. The power of the magnetic field magnified his fear, which in turn warped his DNA. When the process was complete, I couldn't control him. He had the strength of ten men. He was out the door before I could stop him."

"You should have told me. I could have stopped him before he killed anyone. We might have been able to change him back."

Arturo shook his head. "I don't think there was any going back." He adds, "I was too ashamed to tell you."

"Finally, the high priest confesses." I continue to sneer at him. "All your talk doesn't disguise the fact that you experimented on a child before yourself. And that you lied to me, after swearing on the name of your precious God that you would always tell me the truth."

"Everyone lies," he says.

"Guarda cosa sei diventata, Arturo," I say, reverting to the language of his youth, out of frustration, hope. *"Look what's become of you, Arturo."* "When we first met, you wouldn't have hurt a fly. That's why I gave you my blood. I trusted you."

Even on the monitor, I see his gaze is focused in the far distance. My words stir painful memories, for both of us. My hatred for him is matched only by my love. Yes, I still love him, and I hate that about myself. He seems to sense my thoughts for he suddenly glances back at me and smiles. It is a sad smile.

"I cannot defend my acts to you," he replies. "Except to say I thought the rewards of success outweighed the possibility of failure. Yes, I should never have used Ralphe. Yes, I should never have lied to you. But if I had done these things—where would we be today? I'd be long dead in a forgotten grave and you'd be safe and secure in your own selfish universe. We wouldn't have your blood now so we could continue with our noble quest to finish what was started seven centuries ago."

I snicker. "I can't help but notice that you apply the word *selfish* to me. What sickness was magnified in your field when you lay beneath the vibration of my blood? You have become a megalomaniac. You were a priest, a good priest. You used to humble yourself before God. Now you want to be God. If Jesus were alive today, what would you say to him? Or would you give him a chance to explain himself before stealing his blood?"

"Do *you* want a chance to explain yourself?" Arturo asks gently.

"I answer to no man. My conscience is clear."

He raises his voice. I have finally hit a button. "I don't believe you, Sita. Why couldn't you look at me when you accused me of witchcraft?"

"You were a witch! And you haven't changed! Goddamn you, Arturo, can't you see how dangerous it is for me to be held captive by these people? I just have to look at General Havor to know he wants to rule the world."

"He's not the monster *Andy* led you to believe."

"You talk about beliefs. What do you believe in these days? I never met Jesus, it's true. But you must know as well as I that he would never condone your methods. Your lying and ambushing and torture. The means do not justify the end. You did not watch

Ralphe chew on human flesh. If you had seen him, you'd know that this path you want to take stinks of the devil."

Arturo sits back from the screen. He is as tired as I am, perhaps shaken as well. In that moment, his face becomes much older than forty-five. He appears ready for the grave. Yet he is resolved, his destiny will be fulfilled. He shakes his head as he sighs.

"We can do this the hard way, Sita," he says. "Or we can do it the easy way. It is up to you. I need your blood and I am going to have it."

I smile grimly. "Then you'd better prepare yourself for a fight. Let me warn you, Arturo—I've shown you only a fraction of my powers. But if you come after me now, you will see all of them. There aren't enough soldiers and bullets in this compound to contain me for the remainder of my life. Tell your general that people will die if I'm not released. Their deaths will be on your conscience, Arturo. I swear in the name of my God, you will never get to heaven—in this world or the next."

The screen goes dead.

But not before I see the fear in his eyes.

15 ~

More hours pass. Joel lies sleeping. Once again I sit silently on the floor, my legs crossed, my eyes closed. Yet this time my attention is turned outward. Through the wall, I can just hear the guards at the security station talk. There are three of them now. They discuss a football game.

"Those Forty-Niners are amazing," Guard One says. "Their offense works like a machine gun—it just keeps firing. I felt sorry for the Cowboys."

"You know, everybody looks at the quarterback," Guard Two says. "But I think when you got the receivers, you got all you need. Even a lousy pro quarterback can look good throwing to players who are wide open."

"I think it's the other way around," Guard Three says. "You got a great quarterback, he can hit a player who's totally covered. Not many teams win the Super Bowl with an average quarterback."

"Not many teams win the Super Bowl, period," Guard One says.

"Only one a year," Guard Two says.

"Wouldn't be a Super Bowl if everyone could win it," Guard Three says.

Beyond their chattering, I sense their thoughts. The gift of Yaksha's blood grows stronger the more still I become. Guard One is contemplating his sour stomach. He has an ulcer, and when he pulls an all-night shift, it always hurts. He wonders if he should go to his car on the next break and get his bottle of Maalox. But he needs to drink it in private. The other guys always kid him about having a stomachache like a little kid. Actually, Guard One has a lot of guts going into work in the pain he's in.

Guard Two's thoughts are dull. He is thinking about his wife, his current mistress, and a woman he just met in the cafeteria two hours earlier—all of them naked together in bed with him. He drank a large Coke before starting his last shift. He has to pee real bad.

Guard Three is interesting. Unknown to his buddies, he writes science-fiction in his spare time. His brother-in-law, who's a lawyer, just read his last book and told him to forget about becoming a writer. But Guard Three thinks that just because his brother-in-law has a law degree, it doesn't mean he can spot talent. And he's right—Guard Three's mind is rich in creative ideas.

I need to concentrate hard to sense their thoughts. I can only *read* one at a time. Since ancient times I have been able to influence people's thoughts by staring hard at them and whispering suggestions in their ears. But in here I am deprived of the power of my gaze, of the soothing allure of my velvety voice. Yet the longer I concentrate on these guys, the more certain I am that I can introduce thoughts into their minds. I focus in on Guard Three—he's the most sensitive. Creating a strong image in my mind, I send it through the wall.

"This girl is real dangerous. She can kill us all."

Guard Three is saying something that he suddenly breaks off in midsentence. I hear him shift uneasily in his chair. "Hey, guys," he says.

"What?" the other two ask.

"That chick in there is dangerous. We have to be careful with her. You saw what she did to Sam and Charlie."

"She knocked them out cold," Guard Two agrees. "But I'd like to see her try it on me. She wouldn't get far."

"I don't think you want to mess with her," Guard One says. "She's supposed to be super strong."

"Yeah, but they don't tell us why she's strong," Guard Three says. "They just tell us to watch her. But what if she gets out? She could kill us all."

"Yes," I whisper softly to myself.

"Relax," Guard One says. "There's no way she's getting out of that box."

"Even if she does break out," Guard Two says. "We can stop her. I don't care about orders, I'm opening fire."

"I hear bullets can't stop her," Guard Three says, continuing to dwell on how dangerous I am.

I shift my focus to Guard One and send out another suggestion.

"We mustn't lose sight of her."

"We'll keep an eye on her," Guard One says.

I place the same thought in Guard Three's mind.

"Yeah," Guard Three echoes. "We have to be alert, keep watching her."

I try to put the thought in Guard Two's mind.

"I've got to take a piss," Guard Two says.

"Oh, well," I whisper to myself. "Two out of three ain't bad."

Over the next thirty minutes—pausing only when Guard Two goes to the bathroom—I steadily build up their paranoia about how dangerous I am and how bad things will be if they don't keep me under constant surveillance. Pretty soon Guards One and Three are talking paranoid gibberish. Guard Two is not sure how to calm them down, or even *why* they need to be calmed down.

"If we don't watch her every second," Guard One says. "She'll escape."

"And if she escapes," Guard Three says. "She'll rip our hearts out and eat them."

"Stop!" Guard Two yells. "She's not going to escape."

"We know that," Guard One says. "If we don't blink, if we keep the lights on her, she won't escape."

"But if the lights go out, we're doomed," Guard Three says.

"Why would the lights go out?" Guard Two wants to know.

Taking a few deep breaths, I slowly ease out of my deep state of concentration. I reach over and gently shake Joel. He opens his eyes and smiles at me. In all the confusion I have forgotten how handsome he is. His dark blue eyes are filled with affection.

"What a pleasant sight to wake up to," he whispers.

"Thank you."

"Did you sleep?"

I lean over and whisper directly into his ear. "No. I've been planting the seeds of our escape. The guards outside are now terrified of losing sight of us."

He's curious. "You know this for a fact?"

"Yes. I'm going to break the lights in here, which will cause them to panic and call for help. I'm sure General Havor himself will come."

"Then what?"

"I have a plan of sorts, but it's not set in stone. Just follow my lead. Get up—get ready to act when I say the word."

Joel moves to the wall closest to the door. Standing in the center of the cell, staring at the overhead cameras, I give the guards on the other side of the wall one last thing to think about.

"I'm coming for you now," I say in a wicked voice.

"You'd better run, you'd better hide." I lick my lips. "Because I'm *very* hungry."

Then, in a series of blindingly fast moves, I shatter every light on the ceiling and plunge the cell into darkness. I see perfectly, but Joel has to reach for the wall to get his bearings. At the security station, I hear Guard One and Guard Three screaming in terror. Guard Two fumbles for his weapon, yelling at his partners to stop. I suppress a giggle.

"Come to me, General," I whisper. "Come, Arturo."

Five minutes later I hear Arturo and Havor pounding down the narrow hall, speaking heatedly. Although I have not heard the general's voice before, I recognize it by the authority it commands. Arturo has influence within the confines of the compound, but the man with the star on his shoulder is in charge. I wonder about the details of their relationship. All about them, clutching machine guns and trying not to panic, are dozens of soldiers.

"She's not a danger as long as we keep the lock in place," Arturo says to the general. "This is a stunt she's pulling to get us to open the door."

"I don't like it that we can't see her," General Havor snaps back. "You heard what she told you. We don't know the full extent of her powers. For all we know she's cutting through a wall of the cell as we talk."

"She's a master of manipulation," Arturo counters. "She talked about her unknown powers to plant a seed of doubt in our minds—for just this occasion. If you open the door to check on her, she'll be on you in a second. You'll have to kill her to stop her and you can't kill her."

"We'll wait and see what she does next," General Havor says.

"What's happening?" Joel hisses in the dark.

I whisper softly so that only he can hear. "The general and Arturo are coming. They don't want to open the door, but I think I can do something to inspire them to relent. There will be a lot of noise in a few minutes. Besides creating the racket, I will be mentally projecting into the general's mind. Please don't speak to me during this time. I need to concentrate. Then, when they start to open the door, I need you to wedge yourself in the corner behind the door. But don't do it until I give the signal. There'll be gunfire, and the space behind the door will be the safest. Do you understand?"

"Yes. You really think they'll open the door?"

"Yes. I'll make them."

Once more I sit cross-legged on the floor, this time in the center of the room. Quieting my thoughts with several deep breaths, I project myself into the general's mind. It is easy to locate—the psychic energy that emanates from him is like molten lava from an erupting volcano. Yet his resolve will not be so easily manipulated with a few implanted thoughts. With a strong individual, even when I can look him in the eye and whisper in his ear, I have trouble getting him to do what I want. Now, I have neither of those options at my disposal. What I am attempting to do is set up several conditions that will work on the general and prompt him to give the order to open the door. Getting the guards nervous and knocking out the lights were the first of my conditional steps. The next ones will be more difficult.

I slip into General Havor's mind.

It is a black cavern, draped with the webs of poisonous spiders. When he does get my power, I see, General Havor fantasizes about raping me. He also plans to kill Arturo, as soon as the alchemist completes his experiments. There is no trust between the two. General Havor fears Arturo will alter his own DNA and then kill the general. But what Arturo thinks I cannot read. His mind is heavily cloaked— not unexpected in a partial hybrid. Anyway, I must concentrate on the man who gives the orders. General Havor must push the button that opens the door— this is all that matters.

I reach out with my mental claw.

"The witch will break down the door."

I hear the general speak to Arturo.

"Are you positive she cannot break down the door?" he asks.

"Even she cannot destroy this alloy," Arturo reassures him.

"The blood of a dead witch is as good as the blood of a living witch."

General Havor does not speak this thought aloud to Arturo. But I know he fantasizes about shooting me in the head, killing me, and immediately injecting my blood into his veins. It is an attractive idea to him.

Arturo will not be able to stop him, or to come back at him later at an unexpected time, with an unseen dagger in his hand. It is this latter point that is the general's primary worry. My suggestion hits home, and I watch as my mental implant expands and warps. General Havor can almost feel what it will be like to have my blood flow through his veins in the next few minutes. I give the idea another nudge.

"Why wait for the witch's blood?"

Again, General Havor does not share this idea aloud with Arturo.

Still, he is not ready to open the door.

Stretching and breathing normally, I slowly come out of my trance. Enough for mental gymnastics. It is time for brutal force. Climbing to my feet, I study the supposedly impenetrable door, then launch my attack. I leap into the air and plant three extremely powerful kicks on the hard metal with my feet. In quick succession I leap again and again, alternately pounding the door with first my right then my left foot. The door doesn't give, but the noise I create is deafening. Outside I can hear them shouting to one another, and I know what the general is thinking. The witch is going to break out. I may as well open the door and kill her while I have her cornered. To hell with Arturo.

I keep up the pounding.

By this time, I am sure, Guard One and Guard Three have wet their pants.

After five minutes, I pause. Something is happening.

I strain to listen with my ears. General Havor and Arturo are arguing again.

"You are playing right into her hands!" Arturo yells. "The only protection we have from her is this cell. Open it and you open the door to death—both for yourself and your men."

"How long do you think that door can withstand that barrage?" General Havor asks. "See, there are cracks in the walls."

"The cracks are in the walls that hold the metal cage! The cage itself shows no sign of giving."

"I don't believe it!" General Havor snaps. "I say we face her now when we're armed and ready. Better she die than escape."

"But what about her blood? We need it."

"There'll be plenty of her blood lying around when I finish with her."

Arturo hesitates. He lowers his voice. "Plenty of blood for what?"

General Havor does not answer. He knows there will be only enough blood left in my body for him to inject into his own veins. The more I listen to the two, the clearer it becomes that General Havor is not interested in Arturo's hybrid. He wants to be a full-fledged vampire. That's where it's at in his mind.

I return to my pounding.

My feet ache. It doesn't matter.

The noise shakes the whole building.

I imagine even the men in the perimeter towers are trembling.

Outside the door, the guards shout to their general for orders.

General Havor and Arturo continue to argue. I hear them.

"We will die!" Arturo screams.

"She's only one!" General Havor yells. "She can't get us all!" He pauses, makes a decision, and shouts to his men. "Stand ready! We're going in!"

I relax for a moment and catch my breath. "They're coming," I whisper to Joel. "Get behind the door."

"Can't I help?" he asks, moving. "I am a vampire, after all. Not just FBI."

I chuckle softly. "Later, Joel."

Outside, I hear what sounds like a platoon of guards gathering around the red button. Each is more than a little reluctant to push it. The heavy metal door has become awfully comforting. But the general is shouting at them again to open it. Loaded magazines are popped onto M16s. Bullets are locked into firing chambers. Rifles are shouldered. I can smell the sweat of their fear.

Somebody gathers the courage to push the button.

The door begins to open.

I leap up and into a corner near the ceiling.

I don't need to use my newfound levitating abilities. I am able to wedge myself against the ceiling by pressing the back of my neck against one corner wall, and my feet against the other. Supernatural strength has its advantages. I leave my arms free—I am a black widow ready to swoop down and snatch her prey.

They are going to rue the day they decided to lock me in a solid metal cage.

The door opens wider.

I hear them outside in the hall. Their frightened breathing.

You could hear a pin drop. Even without vampire ears.

"She's not there," someone whispers.

They aren't even worried about Joel. Just me, that damn witch.

"She's behind the door," General Havor snarls from farther down the hall.

It's good to know exactly where he is.

"What do we do?" someone croaks. Sounds like Guard Three.

"I'm not going in there," Guard One moans. His ulcer must be killing him.

"I don't like this," Guard Two agrees.

The door will not close again, no matter what happens. I will not let it. But now I am faced with a decision to make. There is only one hostage who will get me to where I want to go, and that is the kind-hearted General Havor. If I abduct Arturo, the general will tell his men to open fire on both of us. Certainly, any guard I would grab would be expendable in the general's mind. Friendly fire, they call it. Yet the general is maybe fifty feet up the hall. Between us are many soldiers. I am going to have to reduce the numbers. I need the men to panic and flee.

I know I will have to cause pain to make that happen.

In a move too swift for the soldiers to see, I slide onto the top of the door, reach outside the cage, grab one of the soldiers by the hair, and pull him back up into the corner with me. The man screams in my hands and I let him carry on for a bit. No doubt he feels like a victim in an *Alien* movie. Because he is crying so loudly, it takes me several seconds to recognize his voice.

It is Guard Three—the one who writes science-fiction in his spare time.

I am sure he has seen *all* the *Alien* movies.

I take his weapon and put my hand over his mouth. "Shh," I whisper. "Things are not so bad as they seem. I am not going to kill you, not if you cooperate. I know about you and I like you. The problem is, I need to scare your friends out there. Now I know they are already pretty spooked, but I've got to get them to the point where they want to flee, no matter what your general orders. Do you understand?"

He nods, his eyes ready to burst out of his head.

I smile. "That's good. They are probably imagining that I am ripping your heart out right now. And with a little help from you, I can make them think that is *exactly* what I am doing. I will hardly have to hurt you at all. Oh, I see you notice I use the word *hurt*. To be honest, I will have to cut you enough so that I can blow the stream of your warm blood out into the hall. Splashing blood always creates a wonderful effect, especially when vampires are involved. While I do that, I want you to scream bloody murder. Can you do that?"

He nods.

I pinch him. "Are you sure?"

"Yes," he croaks. "I don't want to die. I have a wife and two kids."

"I know, and your brother-in-law is a lawyer. By the way, don't listen to a thing he tells you. He is like all lawyers—envious of those who do honest work for a living. You just keep writing your stories. If you want, you can even write one about me. But make me a blond—this red hair is store-bought."

"What's your name?" he asks, relaxing slightly.

I don't want him too relaxed. "I am Mrs. Satan." I scratch him on the inside of his right arm, tearing his flesh and drawing plenty of blood. "Start screaming, buddy."

Guard Three does as he's told. His performance is admirable—he believes half of it. *"Oh God! Stop it! Save me! She's ripping my heart out!"* Actually, he didn't have to get so specific, but I let it pass. While he cries to his fellow soldiers, I purse my lips and blow on the blood that trickles from his arm. I have quite the set of lungs. The blood splatters over the exterior of the wall, and onto the floor outside. I hear the men moaning in horror. This is worse than 'Nam, many think.

They haven't seen anything yet.

"Now let out a real loud death scream," I tell Guard Three. "Trail off into silence. Then, I'll drop you behind the door where my friend is hiding. You might want to stay there when the shooting starts. I warn you ahead of time, I am going to have to kill many of your friends. When I am through, you may leave this building. Get out as fast as you can. Steal a truck if you have to. Things are going to get awfully hot here. Do you understand?"

"Yes. You're not going to kill me?"

"No. Not tonight. You can relax, after you do exactly what I say."

The guard lets out the death scream. I spray an especially wide shower of blood through the doorway. Then I drop the guy down beside Joel, who pats him on the back and tells him to relax. I hand Joel the man's weapon and order him to keep it handy. Several guards outside the door are crying. They have backed away, but not far enough to be safe. I reach out and grab another. He carries a high-powered machine gun, which I wedge between the door and frame. He smells of hamburger and fries. His food is probably not digesting well. I don't know this soldier, which doesn't bode well for him.

"You're going to die now," I tell his horrified face. "I am sorry it has to be this way."

I kill him slowly, painfully, so that his throat-tearing screams and red blood mingle to create an image so ghastly that many of the soldiers feel they are trapped in a nightmare from which they cannot awaken. When I am done, I throw what is left of his body into the hall. It is very messy—the terror in the air is as palpable as the hard metal door that can no longer be closed.

This last execution has disturbed me. If I am forced to kill, I prefer to do so efficiently and painlessly. I will not make another example—I don't have the stomach for it. It is time to leave the building, with Joel and General Havor in hand. To grab the machine gun the soldier brought in, I drop from my position on the ceiling and immediately retrieve it and open fire. The men outside the door stand frozen in place. They fall to their deaths like tenpins.

I kill eight of them before I step into the hall.

Arturo and General Havor are at the far end. They are a hundred feet away and backing up fast. Between us there are many soldiers. I cannot allow the big boss to leave the building without me. But the bloody examples I made of the first two men have had an effect. The soldiers are pushing and crowding behind General Havor and Arturo, slowing them down, preventing them from simply leaving. Also, General Havor has lost control of his men. I stand a clear and easy target in the hallway, but no order to fire comes. In their hearts, the men do not believe this witch can be killed with mere bullets.

They wish they hadn't opened the door.

"Drop your weapons and I will let you live!" I yell.

Most in front of me surrender right then. The few who don't, who take aim, I shoot in the head. The sheer number of deaths does not numb me. I look in the eyes of each one I destroy, and wonder about his life and who he leaves behind. If it was just my life—honestly, if there was no danger of my blood falling into the wrong hands, I would let them cut me down. But I have a responsibility to mankind. I know that is the rationale of every great man or woman, of every merciless monster. The smell of blood is too thick even for my taste.

Arturo and General Havor disappear around the corner.

I call to Joel to join me in the hallway.

He cautiously peeks out. He groans.

"Nothing can be worth this," he whispers.

"You may be right," I say. "Still, we have to get out of here. To do that, we need General Havor."

"Where is he?"

"On the second floor." I grab Joel with my free arm and shield the top of his head with my palm. "Let's join him."

I leap straight up and smash through the ceiling. Again, Yaksha's blood comes to my aid. Without it, such a move would have given me a righteous headache. This time the ceiling barely slows me down. Pulling Joel through the hole I have created, we stand up on the floor of the basement, level one. I see soldiers down the hall jamming the stairs, frantic to exit. Arturo and General Havor struggle in the midst of the human flood. Raising the machine gun to my shoulder, I take aim at General Havor's right thigh. For a split second it is clearly visible. I put a bullet in it. The general stumbles and lets out a cry. No one stops to help him, least of all Arturo. I grab Joel's arm.

"Come," I say.

As I wade into the crowd, they scream and scatter. I guess my red hair does not suit me. Or perhaps it is the fact that I am soaked from head to toe in blood. I must look like a beast that has climbed from the depths of hell. Arturo is already out of sight, but General Havor lies helpless at the side of the stairway. He is lucky that he was not trampled to death. But he is not lucky that it is me who reaches out to help him to his feet.

"General Havor," I say. "Pleased to meet you face to face. Sorry I have to ask a favor so soon after saying hello. But I need you to take me and my friend into the cave behind this compound. I need one of those thermonuclear warheads you keep there. I have a thing about fire, you see, about explosions. For me, the bigger the better."

16

The cave turns into another prison. We reach it without excessive bloodshed, but once inside I am forced to kill all the soldiers. The endless slaughter weighs heavily on me. Joel's broken expression begs me to stop. But I can't stop until it is over, one way or the other. It is my nature never to quit.

We are scarcely inside when the remaining soldiers close the door on us. The metal is as thick as the door on the cell—it cuts in half the miniature rail tracks that run between the compound and the depths of the hill. They also turn off our lights, but there are emergency lanterns. For Joel's sake, and the general's, I turn on several. The stark rays cast ghastly shadows over the carnage I have inflicted. There is blood everywhere. The red blurs in the silent gloom, in my racing mind; it is as if the walls of the cave bleed. I try not to count the dead.

"I didn't want this," I say, pointing my weapon at the general, who sits on the edge of the small railroad car that carries supplies into this place of secrets. His leg continues to bleed but he doesn't complain. He is a horrible human being, but he is not without strength. A hard man with a blunt face, he wears his hair as if it were a disease growing on top of his head. I add, "It's your fault."

My accusation does not faze him. "You can always surrender."

I kneel beside him. To my left Joel sits on the ground, looking weary beyond belief. "But you see that is not an option," I tell the general. "When history started, I was there. And the only reason mankind has been able to move steadily forward is because I have chosen to stand apart from history. I watch what happens. I have no desire to have important roles. Do you understand that I tell you the truth?"

General Havor shrugs. "You've changed your style today."

My voice hardens. "You made me change." I gesture to the dead men who lie around us. "All this is because of you. Look at them. Don't you care about them?"

He is bored. "What do you want? A nuclear bomb?"

I stand and look down at him. "Yes. That's exactly what I want. And after you show it to me, I want you to arm it."

He snorts. "Do you think I'm crazy?"

"I know you're crazy. I have seen inside your mind. I know what you planned to do once you had my blood in your veins. You were going to murder Arturo and rape me."

He's cocky. "You flatter yourself."

I slap him in the face, hard enough to break his nose. "And you sicken me. I don't know how Arturo ever teamed up with you. He must have been desperate. He and I are not alike, by the way. I never beg for anything, but I know how to make you beg. Give me the warhead and arm it or I will subject you to such physical and mental torture you will think that soldier I ripped apart inside the cell died peacefully." I raise my hand to strike again. "Yes?"

He holds his nose; the blood leaks through his thick fingers. "May I ask what you plan to do with the warhead?" he asks.

I catch his eye, push hard enough to make him cower.

"I am going to clean up your mess," I reply.

General Havor agrees to furnish me with a bomb. He digs it out of the back, and wheels it into view on the railroad cart. A black squat affair with a pointed tip and an elaborate control box on the side, it looks like something from an old sci-fi movie. The general informs us that it is rated ten megatons—ten million tons of TNT.

I point to the color-coded buttons on the side.

"Can it be rigged to go off at a specific time?" I ask.

"Yes. It can be set to detonate in ten minutes, or in ten years."

"Ten years is a little long for my tastes. But your men may escape, if they listen to me. You will want to argue my position to them, once we get back outside. Which leads me to my next point." I gesture to the metal wall that blocks the exit. "How do we open this door?"

"It can't be opened from the inside. They've cut our power."

"Is there a radio in here?" Joel asks. "Can you talk to them?"

General Havor shrugs. "I have nothing to say to them."

I grab the general by the collar.

It doesn't take much for him to piss me off.

"You will tell them that we have an armed warhead in here set to detonate in fifteen minutes," I say. "That will be, by the way, the literal truth. You will also inform them that if they wish to prevent the bomb from exploding, they are to let us out. Finally, you will mention that I am willing to negotiate."

He laughs at me. "You can do what you want to me, I am not going to arm this warhead."

I let him go, take a step back. "You think you can play with me, General. You think the worst I can do is kill you. Arturo never told you of the power of my eyes. How my gaze can permanently fry your brain." I pause. "If in the next ten seconds you don't tell me the code to arm this warhead, I will stab such a needle into your forehead that you will have the IQ of a chimpanzee for the rest of your life—however long that may be."

He lowers his head. "I cannot allow you to set off this bomb."

"Very well." I step forward and grab him by the jaw, thrusting his head up, forcing him to stare at me. "Look deep, General! Into the eyes of the witch you thought to control. See where I have prepared a place of fire for you to burn."

17

Ten minutes later the door is opened by the highest
ranking commander on the outside and we wheel a
fully armed warhead into the nighttime air. The
detonator clicks off the seconds. Fifteen minutes to
Armageddon. Driving at high speed should give us
and the soldiers time to get clear of the blast. Overhead, the full moon shines down on our heads,
bathing the entire desert with a milky white radiance.
The setting is dreamlike, as if there has already been a
nuclear explosion, thousands of years ago and the
radioactive fallout remains.

A small army aims a line of high-tech weapons at us.

On all sides, from the guard towers to the rocks in
the hill, we are surrounded.

A minute before, a mumbling General Havor had ordered them to let us go.

But they're not listening.

The highest ranking commander on the outside is now Arturo.

He steps forward as we move out of the cave.

"Sita," he says. "This is madness."

"You tell me about madness, Arturo." I hold a pistol to General Havor's head, shielding myself and Joel with his wobbly figure. He wept as I bored into his brain, but he resisted me as well. I had to destroy most of his mind to get what I wanted. Gesturing to the bomb, I add, "This warhead is set to detonate in less than fifteen minutes. That gives you and your men barely enough time to get clear."

Arturo shakes his head. "We cannot let you escape. An order has come from the President of the United States. At all costs, you are to be stopped." He gestures to the men around us. "We are expendable."

I force a chuckle. "You will not sacrifice all these people."

"It is not my decision to make."

"That's nonsense! They look to you to command them now. Command them to drop their weapons and get the hell out of here." I pause. "You are bluffing."

Arturo looks me in the eye. He is not intimidated by my gaze.

"I pray that you are the one who is bluffing," he says softly.

The timer on the detonator goes to fourteen minutes.

I meet his gaze. "When was the last time you prayed, Arturo? Was it before the inquisitor's court? The day they hanged you? I did what I did then because I know the danger my blood poses for the world. Tonight, I killed all these people for the same reason—to protect humanity."

Arturo challenges me. "To protect us from what? A chance to evolve into something greater? Into creatures that need never grow old, that need never hurt one another? Earlier you laughed at my mission. Seven hundred years ago you also laughed at me. But mine is still the noblest quest on earth—to perfect humanity, to allow it to become godlike."

"You do not become godlike by merging with a monster!"

My words surprise him. "You're not a monster, Sita."

"I am not an angel, either. Or if I am, I am an angel of death—as far as humanity is concerned. True, I have the right to live. Krishna granted me that right. But only if I lived alone, and made no more of my kind. Now I have broken that sacred vow. Krishna will probably judge me harshly. Perhaps he has already judged me, and that is why I am being forced to suffer in this place, to hurt all these people. But what is done is done. I am what I am. Humanity is what it is. We can never join. Don't you see that?"

"Don't you see me, Sita? I am an example of what can be accomplished with a merger of our DNAs. And I am only an incomplete example because I never got to complete the process. Think what mankind can change into if you'll just let me experiment with your blood for the next few weeks. Even a few days would be enough. That's all I'm asking. Then, when I'm finished, I promise to let you go. I will arrange it so that you can go free."

I speak with sorrow. "Arturo, I *can* see you. I see what's become of you. As a young man, you were the ideal person: devout, loving, brilliant. But your brilliance was perverted the day you received my blood. Your love was twisted. For the sake of your experiments, you even sacrificed a boy you loved. You sacrificed us—the love we had for each other. You lied to me, and I think you lie to me again. Your devotion is no longer to Christ—it is to yourself. And even though I have also lied to my God, I still love Krishna and pray he will forgive me for my sins. I still love you, and I pray you will order these people to let us go. But because of both of these loves, I cannot surrender. You cannot have my blood." I pause. "No man can have it."

Arturo knows me.

He knows I'm not bluffing, not when it comes to matters of life and death.

The timer goes to thirteen minutes. Unlucky thirteen.

His face and voice show his resignation. "I cannot let you go," he says quietly.

I nod. "Then we will stand here until the bomb goes off."

Joel looks at me. I stare silently at Joel. There are no words left.

Arturo stands still as a statue. The moon shines down.

Twelve. Eleven. Ten.

Ten minutes might be long enough to get clear of the blast.

"Arturo, ti prego," I say suddenly. *"Arturo, please."* "At least warn your men. Let them flee. I have enough blood on my conscience."

"The blast will leave no blood," he says, turning his eyes upward, toward the sky. "We will be like dust, floating on the wind."

"That is fine for you and me. We have lived long lives. But most of these men are young. They have families. Give the order—enough will remain to prevent Joel and me from escaping."

Arturo sighs and turns. He raises his arms and shouts. "Units G and H are free to go! Hurry! A nuclear bomb is about to detonate!"

There is a great commotion. I suspect more than units G and H want to leave. The men pour into their trucks. Engines roar to life. Tires burn rubber. The front gate is thrown open. The vehicles roar out of sight. Driving at a hundred miles an hour, they can put at least twelve miles between themselves and the blast in the time they have left. They should survive. Yet many remain behind who will not survive. Too many men still stand guard over us. If we try to escape, we will be cut down. It is better to go out like this, I think. Standing on our feet. Disintegrating in an all-consuming wave of fire.

Then I remember something.

"He's in a box so thick an atomic bomb couldn't blast through it."

But if we move and try to flee toward the lab basement, they'll open fire.

For the first time in my long life, I can see no way out.

Time creeps by.

Eight. Seven. Six. Five.

"I don't even know if the warhead can be deactivated once it's armed," I mutter.

"It can't be," General Havor mumbles with what is left of his mind.

"Oh," I say.

Then I begin to feel a peculiar sensation, a subtle but constant vibration inside my body. The moon is directly overhead, of course. It has been shining down on us since we left the cave. But what I didn't realize—with all that was going on around me—was that the moonlight has been filling my body all the time we have been out in the open. It has become more and more transparent. I feel as if I am made of glass. Interesting, I think—and I didn't even have to take my clothes off. It is Arturo who is the first one other than myself to notice the effect.

"Sita!" he cries. "What's happening to you?"

Standing beside me, Joel gasps. "I can see through you!"

I let go of the general. Staring down at my hands, I glimpse the ground through my open palms, through my fingers. Yet I can still see the blood pulsing in my veins, the tiny capillaries glowing like a complex web of fiber optics. A cool energy sweeps over me, yet my heart is strangely warmed.

It warms even as it starts to break.

The white glow spreads around me.

I realize I can just lift off and fly away.

Yaksha's blood, maybe Krishna's grace, gives me another chance.

Do I want it? I feel myself leave the earth.

I reach out to hug Joel, to carry him away with me.

My arms go right through him!

"Joel," I cry. "Can you hear me?"

He squints. "Yes, but it's hard to focus on you. What's going on? Is this a special vampire power?"

My luminous body floats a foot off the ground now.

"It is a gift," I say. Despite my unusual physical state, I feel tears on my face, white diamonds that sparkle with a red sheen as they roll over my transparent cheeks. Once more, I have to say goodbye to those whom I love. "It is a curse, Joel."

He smiles. "Fly away, Sita, far away. Your time is not over."

"I love you," I say.

"I love you. The grace of God is still with you."

The ground is two feet below me now. Arturo tries to grab me, but can't. He stands back and shakes his head, resigned.

"You are probably right," he says. "Mankind is not ready for this." He adds, "Everything you require is in my basement. It is your choice."

I don't understand. But I smile at him as I float higher.

THE LAST VAMPIRE 3: RED DICE

"Ti amo," I whisper.

"Ti amo anch'io, Sita."

A wind takes hold of me. Suddenly I am soaring. The stars shine around me. The moon beats down on the top of my head like an alien sun spawned in the center of a distant galaxy. It is so bright! My now-invisible eyes can hardly bear the glare, and I am forced to close them. As I do an even greater light ignites beneath me. The fiery rays of it rise up and pierce through my etheric body. There is tremendous heat and noise. A shock wave as thick as a granite mountain strikes me. Yet I feel no pain—just swept away, on currents of destruction and tidal waves of death. The compound is gone, the stolen blood is vapor. The world is safe once again. But I, Sita, I am lost in the night.

Epilogue

There is, to my utter amazement, a basement in Arturo's Las Vegas home. The afternoon after the atomic blast, I peer through the carefully hidden trapdoor and discover sheets of copper, magnetic crosses arranged in odd angles, and, most important of all, an empty crystal vial, waiting to be filled with blood. A mirror rests above the vial. It can reflect either the sun or the moon, depending on how much you want to wager.

I call Seymour Dorsten, explain the possibilities to him.

Wait, he cautions. He is on his way.

I sit down and wait. Time passes slowly.

"Everything you require is in the basement."

Do I still want a daughter? Do I still crave immortality?

Deep questions. I have no answers.

Seymour arrives and tries to talk me out of it.

Being human is not so great, he says.

Being a vampire gets old, I counter.

I know that I will attempt the transformation.

But I need some of his blood.

Make me a vampire first, he pleads.

That will not work, I remind him.

But, he protests.

The answer is no, I say firmly.

I take his blood, fill the vial to the brim, then tell him to get lost.

When the sun is at its peak, I lie down on the copper sheets.

The magnets draw out my aura. The magic begins.

When I awake, I feel weak and disoriented. Someone is knocking at the door. I have to struggle up the steps to answer it. There is a spongy texture to my skin I have never noticed before, and my vision is blurred. I am not even sure where I am—only that it is dark. Blood pounds in my head, and I feel I will be sick.

I reach the front door.

A shadow moves outside the glazed side window panel.

Just before I open the door, I remember everything.

"Am I human?" I whisper to myself.

Yet I am not given a chance to know.

The knocking continues.

"Who is it?" I call in a hoarse voice.

"It's your darling," the person replies.

Odd. It doesn't sound like Seymour.

Yet the voice is familiar. From long ago.

But the tone is a little demanding. Sort of impatient.

"Open the door," the person calls.

I wonder if I should.

Staring down at my trembling hands, I wonder many things.

TO BE CONTINUED . . .

Look for Christopher Pike's

The Lost Mind

Coming mid-July 1995

About the Author

CHRISTOPHER PIKE was born in Brooklyn, New York, but grew up in Los Angeles, where he lives to this day. Prior to becoming a writer, he worked in a factory, painted houses, and programmed computers. His hobbies include astronomy, meditating, running, playing with his nieces and nephews, and making sure his books are prominently displayed in local bookstores. He is the author of *Last Act, Spellbound, Gimme a Kiss, Remember Me, Scavenger Hunt, Final Friends* 1, 2, and 3, *Fall into Darkness, See You Later, Witch, Die Softly, Bury Me Deep, Whisper of Death, Chain Letter 2: The Ancient Evil, Master of Murder, Monster, Road to Nowhere, The Eternal Enemy, The Immortal, The Wicked Heart, The Midnight Club, The Last Vampire, The Last Vampire 2: Black Blood, The Last Vampire 3: Red Dice, Remember Me 2: The Return, Remember Me 3: The Last Story, The Lost Mind, The Visitor, The Last Vampire 4: Phantom, The Last Vampire 5: Evil Thirst, The Last Vampire 6: Creatures of Forever, The Starlight Crystal, The Tachyon Web, Execution of Innocence, Tales of Terror #1, The Star Group, The Hollow Skull,* and *Tales of Terror #2*—all available from Archway Paperbacks. *Slumber Party, Weekend, Chain Letter,* and *Sati*—an adult novel about a very unusual lady—are also by Mr. Pike.

"Well, we could grind our enemies into powder with a sledgehammer, but gosh, we did that last night."
— XANDER

BUFFY

THE VAMPIRE

SLAYER ™

As long as there have been vampires, there has been the Slayer. One girl in all the world, to find them where they gather and to stop the spread of their evil ... the swell of their numbers.

#1 THE HARVEST

#2 HALLOWEEN RAIN

#3 COYOTE MOON

#4 NIGHT OF THE LIVING RERUN

THE ANGEL CHRONICLES, VOL. 1

BLOODED

THE WATCHER'S GUIDE
(The Totally Pointy Guide for the Ultimate Fan!)

THE ANGEL CHRONICLES, VOL. 2

Based on the hit TV series created by Joss Whedon

Published by Pocket Books

1399-08
TM & © by Twentieth Century Fox Film Corporation. All Right Reserved.